Rebecca Brandewyne

Shannon Drake

Jill Gregory

Becky Lee Weyrich

The night is a haunted and mysterious realm of shadows—where nothing is impossible... and love is the strangest, most powerful magic of all.

Prepare for an unforgettable journey far beyond the boundaries of dreams and desires— as an acclaimed quartet of your favorite romance writers transports you to breathtaking new heights of sensuous, supernatural ecstasy ...and to the miraculous places in the heart where the most secret, cherished wishes always come true.

Avon Books Presents

Night Magic

REBECCA BRANDEWYNE
SHANNON DRAKE • JILL GREGORY
BECKY LEE WEYRICH

AVON BOOKS ◆ NEW YORK

AVON BOOKS PRESENTS: NIGHT MAGIC is an original publication of Avon Books. This work, as well as each individual story, has never before appeared in print. This work is a collection of fiction. Any similarity to actual persons or events is purely coincidental.

AVON BOOKS
A division of
The Hearst Corporation
1350 Avenue of the Americas
New York, New York 10019

Published by arrangement with the authors
Library of Congress Catalog Card Number: 93-90235
ISBN: 0-380-76812-7

First Avon Books Printing: September 1993

AVON TRADEMARK REG. U.S. PAT. OFF. AND IN OTHER COUNTRIES, MARCA REGISTRADA, HECHO EN U.S.A.

Printed in the U.S.A.

RA   10 9 8 7 6 5 4 3 2 1

Contents

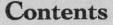

Moonstruck

Rebecca Brandewyne

For Sandy Kennedy,
in appreciation for her friendship
and her assistance in making this story happen.

In Ireland did Ceann-Tìre,
A massive castle dark as he
Who was its lord and master, rise
Where sea gulls flew against the skies
Over a sunless sea.
There, twice five miles of rocky ground
With walls and towers were girdled round;
And there were dungeons damp with sinuous chills,
Where torches cast many a shadow eerie;
And, beyond, were forests ancient as the hills,
Enfolded by misted vales of greenery.

But oh! that soaring promontory that slanted
Up from the cobbled causeway with frothy cover!
A savage place! as hellish and enchanted
As e'er beneath a pale full moon was haunted
By woman crying for her bestial lover!
The howling of the wind through there
Shouted a warning Beware! Beware—
His amber eyes, his ebon hair!
Weave a circle round him thrice,
And close your eyes with holy dread,
For he on honey-dew hath fed
And drunk the milk of Paradise.

Amid the standing stones of glade
To bewitching bride, he laid claim.
Moonstruck was he, damned, accursed;
To be free of madness must he e'er thirst,

2

Or was she the one, a healing flame,
A blessed fire of eternal light,
E'er to illuminate his long, dark night,
With heart that burned, a splendorous glow,
Strong and certain of its power to tame
The wilder half she would come to know?
No curse, but gift is love by any name!

—Adapted from *Kubla Khan, or, A Vision in a Dream*
by Samuel Taylor Coleridge

Prologue

Ulster, Ireland
Date unknown

Witch, the O'Neill had called her as he had bound her securely to the stout post his men had erected at the heart of the ancient standing stones. At her feet, the men had piled tinder and thorny branches from the trees and brambles of the forest, and the O'Neill himself had thrust into the fagots the lighted torch that had set them afire. Now, beneath the full moon that eerily illuminated the shadowy glade where the stone ring stood, he and his men snarled and prowled like a pack of predators, cloaked in their animal skins against the wintry chill that Igrania no longer felt as the flames blazed high. She thought of her beloved husband and newborn babe, from whom her enemies had abducted her, and of the O'Neill's weight upon her when he had pressed her down to slake his lust upon her; and tears stung her smoke-blinded eyes for all she had known and lost because she was a Kilclare and beautiful, and the O'Neill had wanted her.

"I curse you," she gasped with her last, dying breath, coughing as the acrid smoke filled her lungs. "I curse you, O'Neill, Lord of Ceann-Tìre, and all your descendants. Henceforth, let this night be what you have made of it . . . and you what you have become in your wickedness; and this you shall be until even a woman such as I shall know you are more . . . So I, Igrania of Clare Caiseal, do curse you . . . "

The wind carried away her words, and then her ashes. But her cryptic curse remained to plague the O'Neill and his men; and ever after, believing that only a woman of Igrania's blood could rescind the curse, the men of the Clan O'Neill of Clandeboye, who from that time hence were afflicted by a mysterious malady that none dared name, sought by whatever means they could to take as captives women of the Clan Kilclare. The Kilclares never knew what befell these unfortunate women, only that none was ever heard from again. Surely upon the women, the O'Neills wreaked pain and suffering in revenge for their accursedness—though this did not gain their release from it.

So the feud between the two clans was born; the wheel of time turned, and the standing stones grew ever more weathered and aged, falling prey to the elements and time's ravages. The menhirs leaned ever farther from their original upright positions, and the top slabs of some of the dolmens crashed down upon the earth and broke in two. Inevitably perhaps, the clearing in the woods where the stones stood became known as a haunted place; and people swore that on a night when the moon rose full in the sky and the wind howled across the land, the stones themselves came alive and whispered, "I curse you . . . "

1

Ulster, Ireland
1470

As swift as a wolf in pursuit of fleeing prey, the twilight came, sullen and clammy, cloaked with clouds of mist that billowed in from the sea to the east, where frothy waves churned and pounded and broke upon bleak shores. From the beach, the dusk and mist wove cold, hoary strands across the sweeping moors and through the aged, gnarled trees of the darkling glens beyond, and wound like a shroud about the towering mountains that hove up against the western horizon. Upon the caparisoned procession wending its way on horseback along the narrow, muddy track that snaked through the forested vales, drizzle spattered from the thunderheads massed in the firmament, making the torches that the men carried sizzle and spit.

"Sure and 'tis an evening fit for naught save beguilement or butchery—and the damned O'Neills of Clandeboye be practitioners of both!" one of the men muttered uneasily, both angry and afraid. Shuddering, he glanced back over his shoulder before making the ancient sign against evil. "Methinks 'tis like as not we be riding into a trap laid by those demon's spawn!"

Among the man's companions sounded grum-

blings of accord. Still, none of them dared to suggest
that they turn back, for both the brave and cowardly
among them feared the wrath of their leader, their
chief, the *tòiseach** of Clare Caiseal, Lord Tadhg Kilclare, even more than they feared the treachery and
savagery of the Clan O'Neill of Clandeboye. So they
were careful to ensure that their complaints did not
reach the ears of the grim, gray-bearded giant of a
man who rode at their vanguard.

Among them all, only *he*, the Kilclare, was una-
fraid of either ambush or atrocity on this inauspi-
cious eve, his face as sternly set and purposeful as
it had been a fortnight ago when he had learned of
his kinsman Ruaidhri's capture by the Clan O'Neill
and the terms demanded for the hostage's release.
In exchange for Ruaidhri's life and freedom, his betrothed, the Kilclare's daughter, Sionna, must be delivered up to the Clan O'Neill, to become the bride
of Lord Lucan O'Neill, the *tòiseach* of Ceann-Tìre.

But for all that the Kilclare's resolve to sacrifice
his only child was merciless and unyielding, his
fierce black eyes trained sharply on the rough, dimly
lighted road that twisted away into the ever-
deepening shadows stretching before the procession,
he could not help but be aware of the young woman
who rode at his side, of the fear and rage and silent
accusation that emanated from her slender, cloaked
figure mounted atop a pure-white mare as lovely
and spirited and fine-boned as she.

Lady Sionna Kilclare sat straight and tall in the
saddle, her chin held high. Like her stalwart father,
she looked neither right nor left, her attention fixed
on the path, not only to see it more clearly in the
increasing darkness, but also to hide the tears of
fright and fury that glistened in her wide, luminous,

*See Gaelic Glossary on page 105 for definitions of all Gaelic words.

sloe eyes. Inside the ermine-trimmed hood of her sable mantle, her face was as white as the foam that crowned the distant sea, her hair as black as a night that had swallowed the moon and stars. The contrast was startling, striking; yet Sionna had never found joy in the renowned fairness that, together with her lineage, had made her such a coveted marriage prize. Instead, her beauty and blue blood were the bane of her existence, shackling her first to her kinsman Ruaidhri, whom she bore no love, and now to Lord Lucan O'Neill of Clandeboye, whose very name she dreaded and despised.

Sionna's heart cried out in protest when she thought of being the O'Neill's wife. At least Ruaidhri was her kinsman; but the O'Neills had been the Kilclares' mortal enemies for centuries and, worse, lay under a curse delivered upon them by one of Sionna's own ancestors, Igrania of Clare Caiseal. Like most, Sionna had heard only whispered rumors about the curse, of how it had driven its victims to madness and monstrosity. But whether this was indeed so, she did not know; for even more terrifying than these grisly stories was the fact that even under torture, no man of the Clan O'Neill of Clandeboye had ever revealed the bane's true nature. Nor did Sionna know how to rescind the curse, and she trembled to think what would befall her when this hapless truth was revealed; for to cure his affliction must be why the O'Neill wanted her badly enough to wed her, knowing he would not get a *tòiseach*'s daughter as a whore, not even in exchange for so valuable a hostage.

That her own father had condemned her to this fate worse than death was not to be borne. But bear it she must, Sionna knew. Deep down inside, she had known it from the beginning, when the messenger clad in the colors of the Clan O'Neill had appeared in the great hall of her father's castle to boast of Ruaidhri's capture and to present the terms demanded for the hostage's release.

"Nay! Ruaidhri can rot in Ceann-Tìre's dungeons or rot in hell, for all I care! I do not love him—and I will enter a convent, I swear, ere, to save his bloody neck, I marry an accursed O'Neill of Clandeboye!" Sionna had cried.

But even as she had railed against the miserable tidings and her grievous misfortune, she had known there was no escape for her. Her father had no sons. Ruaidhri was the *tànaiste* of Clare Caiseal. As both her father's second-in-command and heir, he was far more valuable than she, a mere woman. She would be handed over to the O'Neills and mourned as one dead by the Kilclares.

Now, Sionna shuddered violently at the thought, drawing her cape more closely about her to ward off the chill that had settled deep in the marrow of her bones. She felt frozen with both cold and terror at the prospect not only of marrying a stranger, a fiendish enemy, but also, far worse, of being forced to lie with him; for she did not deceive herself that on this, his wedding night, the O'Neill would be denied his rights as her husband. Although silently, earnestly, she prayed he would be kind and gentle and merciful, the gruesome tales she had heard about his clan seemed to preclude that; Sionna expected and feared he would use her brutally. For that, she damned both her father and Ruaidhri.

As the procession pressed on with grim determination, her mount stumbled upon a slick, entangled patch of ground, nearly unseating her from the saddle. Her gloves were soaked through, her hands like ice upon the reins, and not even a sliver of moonlight shimmered through the trees to help illuminate the track that twined before her; for the appointed night of the exchange was the dark of the moon. The

O'Neill himself had insisted on this, Sionna had been told, and she shivered again at this hint of his wicked, macabre nature.

For a wild, desperate moment, she was tempted to lash her mare to flight, to plunge from the road into the forest, where she would be swallowed by the mist and trees and darkness, lost to those who would pursue her. But such an act would not only shame her father, but also cost Ruaidhri his life; and these things, Sionna could not bring herself to do, not even to save herself.

Still, her heart lurched in her breast when she spied the torches glimmering like will-o'-the-wisps ahead in the distance, for she knew that the fire-brands belonged to the O'Neills of Clandeboye—as she herself would belong to them before this dire night was done.

Sensing both the interlopers and the growing trep-idation of their mistress, the two huge gray wolf-hounds that trotted at Sionna's side, Marhalt and Maeve, growled deep in their throats; and for the first time since the tearful parting from her mother earlier that eve, Sionna spoke, softly bidding the dogs to be silent. Obediently, they quieted, although they remained alert and wary, ready to spring to her defense; and she drew comfort from them. She had raised them from pups and intended that they should accompany her to Ceann-Tìre. Surely, the O'Neill would permit her that single solace, Sionna thought anxiously, biting her generous lower lip at the knowledge that perhaps he would not, and there would be naught she could do about it. By law, a wife was chattel, the property of her husband, and had no rights of her own. Once she was his, the O'Neill could do whatever he pleased with her, *to* her, and she would be helpless to prevent it.

It was this that terrified Sionna most of all, the fact

that at Ceann-Tìre, she would be totally alone, cut off from the entire Clan Kilclare, powerless against the O'Neill and his kinsmen, with none to speak for her, none to lift a hand in her defense. Even her faithful serving maid, Brigid, Sionna had left behind at Clare Caiseal, unable to condemn another to share her fate.

Still, however much she might wish otherwise, there was no turning back from the road she traveled; for now, causing her heart to leap to her throat, the mist suddenly shifted like a gossamer veil drawn aside by spectral hands to reveal the haunted glade that the accursed O'Neill had designated as the neutral ground for the meeting between his clan and hers.

Set into the earth, torches blazed all around the ring of ancient gray stones that stood in the middle of the clearing and so marked it as a place of pagan ceremony and blood sacrifice. At the center of the menhirs and dolmens, a solitary stone lay like an altar, and upon this was spread a magnificent Oriental carpet in deep, rich hues. Above it hung a fringed canopy of resplendent cloth of gold mounted on four brass poles driven into the ground at each corner. Upon one end of the carpet stood an actual chapel altar, intricately carved and gilded and draped with an elaborately embroidered altar cloth. On this sat a silver chalice and ciborium chased with priceless gemstones and flanked by a pair of matching silver candelabra. The dozen pure-white beeswax candles of the candelabra were alight and fluttered wildly in the wind, as though at any moment they would be extinguished. Before the altar were two kneeling pillows of burgundy brocade that appeared chillingly like stains of blood once spilled upon the monolith, remnants of some idolatrous ritual of old.

Adding to the mystique of this tableau were the

men arrayed around it. Clad in the colors of the Clan O'Neill of Clandeboye, they bristled so with glittering weapons and gleamed so with ancient Celtic jewelry that they themselves appeared like heathens in the torchlight, gathered for some primitive rite. Sionna half suspected that beneath their fur cloaks and armor, some if not all the men were tattooed with blue woad; for numbered among the ancestors of the O'Neills were the dark Cruthni who had settled in Scotland across the eastern sea, a tribe the ancient Romans had called the Picti, meaning "painted." The knowledge that, from this night forward, these were to be her kinsmen filled Sionna with greater fear. Surely, the dark rumors whispered about them must be true! For despite the holy elements they had brought to it, their choosing of this haunted, pagan place for her wedding ceremony seemed so profane, as though she herself were to be sacrificed upon the monolith at the heart of the standing stones, as though it were the devil himself she was to marry.

No sooner had these disturbing thoughts crossed her mind than Sionna's attention was abruptly caught and held by a man who stood a little apart from the rest, at the fringe of the black-shrouded trees, watching her intently; somehow, even before he approached her, she knew he was the O'Neill, the lord and master to whom she would this night unwillingly give her troth and virtue. Unwittingly, she gasped when he stepped from the shadows into the erratic torchlight; for although she had been informed that the O'Neill was neither old nor repellent in appearance, she had not expected this tall, dark, powerful man in his prime who, with the sinuous grace of a prowling beast, now stalked her, his face and form at once so brutal and yet so compellingly handsome that he was spellbinding to behold.

Standing well over six feet, he had massive shoulders, arms bulging with muscles, and a broad chest that tapered to a firm, flat belly; taut, narrow hips, and thick, corded thighs. Yet unlike other men of such great size, there was nothing slow or ponderous about him. He tread lightly, lithely, his footfalls scarcely making any sound, his muscles fluid, rippling with obvious strength and agility. He was like some dangerous wild animal metamorphosed into a man, Sionna thought, disquieted—primal, savage, predatory. Yet despite herself, she could not tear her eyes from him as, acknowledging no one else, not even her father, he strode to stand before her, one hand stretching out to capture her mare's bridle, making its silver trappings jingle overloud in the tense silence.

No greetings were exchanged. All those present were fully aware of the unsavory purpose of this meeting; and knowing, as well, that any sudden movement might set off a bloody battle between the two feuding clans, the others in the clearing were still, their attention fastened on the predominant male who appeared to cause all about him to dwindle into insignificance. Sionna was no longer even aware of the rest. Such was the man's undeniable, atavistic appeal that it was as though he and she were alone in the glade, her senses focused so narrowly, so acutely, on him that even the inhospitable elements seemed to fade into the night.

His thick, shaggy, shoulder-length hair, as black and glossy as the pelt of some sleek beast and glistening with rain where touched by the flare of the firebrands, rippled and streamed back in the wind to reveal a hard, dark-stubbled bronze visage stamped with such bold, brutishly beautiful features that he looked even more barbaric than his men. His heavy black brows swooped like the widespread

wings of a raven above intense, deep-set eyes that
held Sionna spellbound as they slowly raked her
quivering figure, then riveted on her ashen face ob-
scured by the hood of her mantle. She had never
before seen such eyes on a man; like those of an
animal in the night, they glowed a startling shade of
amber and seemed to pierce to her very soul. Involuntarily, she shrank deeper into the warm, conceal-
ing folds of her cape, as though they might offer
some protection against him. At that, the nostrils of
his chiseled Roman nose flared, and a wolfish smile
curved his full, carnal mouth, as though he scented
her fear and were amused by it.

Then, before Sionna realized what he intended,
the man reached up and swept her from the saddle,
his strong hands like an iron band girding her wil-
lowy waist. Such was the potency of the unexpected
tremor that jolted her at his touch that she instinctively struggled to wrest free of him. But his grip
was too powerful, too secure; with the merest flex
of the muscles that corded his brawny arms, he easily restrained her, his hold upon her so painful that
she knew she would have bruises from it tomorrow.
Discerning her fear and impotence against him, Marhalt and Maeve, snarling and snapping, would have
sprung to her defense. But much to her astonishment
and alarm, before Sionna could stay their attack, the
man himself barked a sharp directive, and the wolfhounds fell back upon their haunches. That the dogs
should cower before him filled Sionna with panic,
for he should not have been able to warn them off.
Here was proof indeed of his fiendishness; and she
shuddered uncontrollably in his grasp, wishing fervently that he would release her.

He did not. Instead, for a seemingly endless moment, he held her close against the hard-muscled
length of his huge, strong, supple body, so close that

she thought he must surely feel the frantic pounding of her heart against his, sense the strange turmoil she felt inside at his diabolic touch, her loathing and longing to escape from him. But if he did, these things mattered not to him.

With the assurance of a man who knew she was his for the taking, the O'Neill slowly slid his hands up her cloak to push back its cowl, exposing her fair countenance. She heard the hiss of his sharply indrawn breath at the sight of her; and then, when she mutely, stubbornly refused to meet his gaze, Sionna felt the steeliness of his hand beneath her chin, forcing her face up to his. Her midnight-blue eyes sparked with ire at this further display of his dominance over her; crimson stained her high cheekbones. Once more, she attempted to jerk away from him, and once more, he curbed her, compelling her to turn her face so it was clearly illuminated by the torchlight. Glancing then toward one of his men— the messenger, Cullach O'Neill, who had come to her father's castle—the O'Neill was assured by his kinsman's quick nod of agreement that Sionna was indeed the daughter of the Kilclare and not another woman deceptively substituted in her place. Then, looking back at her, the O'Neill at last spoke.

"I am Lucan O'Neill of Clandeboye, my lady," he announced in a low, mellifluous voice, "lord and master of Ceann-Tìre—as I will be lord and master of you also, my reluctant bride, ere this night is done."

The last words were soft, cavalier, mocking, intended to frighten and to humiliate her, Sionna realized, incensed. He trailed his fingers provocatively down her swanlike throat, then tightened them there briefly, to make clear his strength and supremacy. Fury roiled within her. Recklessly, she raised her hand to slap the insolent smile from his brutal, handsome face and succeeded only in feeling the harsh bite of his fingers around her wrist as his own hand shot out swiftly to check her assault. Such was the pressure of his hold upon her that with a sob, she caught her breath, tears stinging her eyes.

"Faith, but you dare much, my lady, for a woman soon to be at my utter mercy. By God, there's no man alive would lift a hand to me—and live," the O'Neill asserted arrogantly, both his tone and the muscle throbbing in his determined, set jaw warning Sionna of the wrath he restrained with difficulty. "You are, in truth, as Cullach told me, as boldly spirited as you are uncommonly beautiful, and while that does not wholly displease me, neither does it allay my deep-rooted suspicion that you would sooner stab a *sgian-dubh* into my back than call me husband."

"Aye, and so I shall be doing, my lord, given half the chance!" Sionna vowed fiercely, even as she cursed her unruly tongue, for surely now the O'Neill would strike her for her impudence. Her father had often done so, as had Ruaidhri in the past. Recoiling from the memory, she involuntarily steeled herself to receive the punishing blow.

"So . . . you are not unaware of what it is to be beaten by a man," the O'Neill observed as he noted her anxious, watchful eyes, her cringing, guarded posture. "A circumstance that hardly surprises me, given your obvious rebellious temperament. That 'tis yet so pronounced is no credit to your kinsmen; they've done you no favor, I assure you. Far better that they had taught you a woman's place from the beginning—as I intend to do—for 'tis a hard lesson you'll be learning now. So if you are wise, you will mark my words well, my lady: Try me not, for I am no more patient or gentle than any other man; and I'll brook no challenge to my authority." He paused, allowing this warning to penetrate. Then he continued more quietly, jeeringly, "Still, though I confess you tempt me sorely, when I do this night lay hands upon you, 'twill not be to thrash you, my lady, but for a much sweeter purpose, I promise you."

The O'Neill's hypnotic golden eyes smoldered like twin embers as they swept the length of her lingeringly, thoroughly, in a way that left no possible doubt as to his meaning. Sionna blanched as though he had indeed hit her. Now that she had seen him, the thought of lying with this man was even more terrifying. There emanated from the O'Neill a seductive aura of animal magnetism and menace that was so powerful as to be almost tangible. He was clearly a man accustomed to demanding—and getting—what he wanted; and she sensed he would not be content, as Ruaidhri would have been, merely with taking her, while she lay still and submissive beneath him. Rather, the O'Neill would be driven by a raw, primal male need to conquer and to dominate and to possess her absolutely; and she would be lost, utterly helpless against him. Sionna trembled as she unwittingly envisioned him pressing her down and invading her; and, stricken, she lowered her eyes, her cheeks coloring at the thought of the intimacies this man would presently force upon her.

"I see that you understand me, my lady," the O'Neill drawled derisively, with satisfaction at this evidence of her modesty and maidenly apprehension. "Let us hope you are, in truth, as virtuous as your demeanor now suggests, for 'tis not deceived and cheated I'll be by taking Ruaidhri's leavings, but paid in full the price owed me for his life and freedom. That being so, you would do well, my lady, to speak now if you have bestowed upon him what by all rights belongs to me, for otherwise, you shall suffer greatly for it, I swear."

"Have mercy, my lord," Sionna beseeched softly, "for on my oath, I am yet chaste."

Though she spoke truly, yet did she shudder at the thought that perhaps there would be no proof of this claim when the O'Neill took her. She had heard that sometimes there was not, though a woman be as pure as the day she was born; and she knew the atrocities to which a husband might subject a bride for coming sullied to his bed.

"Then, come, my lady," the O'Neill demanded imperiously, interrupting Sionna's distressing reverie and, when she would have hung back, taking her hand in his to haul her toward the chapel altar on the monolith. "The hour grows late, the priest awaits, and we've a long ride yet ahead of us in this foul weather to Ceann-Tíre." Then, glancing toward his men, he called sharply, "Bring the hostage forward—and if the Lady Sionna fails even once to respond properly during the ceremony, slay him!"

At that, cursing and struggling mightily against both the O'Neills on either side of him and the rope that bound his wrists cruelly behind his back, Ruaidhri was roughly dragged from the edge of the trees into the clearing. By the unsteady light of the firebrands, Sionna saw that he had been mercilessly battered. His face was cut and bruised, encrusted with scabs born of older wounds wreaked during his imprisonment; his nose was broken, and one eye was nearly swollen shut. Blood from a fresh gouge upon his forehead streamed down his cheek in the rain, and he walked with a pronounced limp. Yet when she thought of what she herself must endure for his foolishness in allowing himself to be taken prisoner by the O'Neills of Clandeboye, Sionna could not find it in her tortured heart to pity him. Upon his release, Ruaidhri's wounds would heal; what were a few gashes and lumps compared to the violation and degradation *she* would suffer at the hands of the O'Neill, from whom there would be no escape, ever?

At Ruaidhri's appearance, Sionna's father and kinsmen finally dismounted; she recognized, bitterly, that it was only now, when they were certain Ruaidhri was actually present in the glade, that they were willing to put themselves at risk among the O'Neills by giving up the advantage of being on horseback. Not even for her, the Kilclare's daughter, had they been disposed to do so before. The realization hurt deeply, and Sionna's eyes flashed like sapphires as they met Ruaidhri's own tormented emerald-green ones. *He* was to blame for her misfortune; if not for him, she would not be here now. She had never loved him, had never wanted to marry him. How ironic that now, to save his life, to gain his freedom, she must wed another, an enemy, in his stead.

Spying Sionna, and knowing from the earlier taunts of his captors why she was there, Ruaidhri swore even more furiously and fought all the harder against his bonds and the men who restrained him, to no avail. He was prodded by the keenly honed point of a *sgian-dubh* to kneel upon the soaked earth and to lay his head upon a wooden block that one of the O'Neill's men, with a barbed jest and a crude laugh, placed before him. Beside Ruaidhri's ignominiously bent figure, Cullach O'Neill now stood, *claidheamh mór* in hand, its long, broad silver blade, engraved with runes, glinting wickedly in the torchlight, poised to sever Ruaidhri's head from his body if Sionna misspoke her marriage vows.

"I forbid you to wed him, *cailin*! I forbid you, do you hear?" Ruaidhri shouted hoarsely to Sionna as the O'Neill pulled her onto the monolith to stand before the chapel altar beneath the cloth-of-gold canopy, which, sodden with rain, flogged wildly in the wind. "I'd rather be dead and in hell than live to see you married to the likes of that accursed devil!"

"Aye, and straight to hell is where I'll surely be sending you, you bloody bastard, if you don't shut your damned trap!" With the heavy hilt of his claymore, Cullach delivered such a vicious clout to Ruaidhri's skull that an audible crack rang out through the clearing.

An involuntary cry issued from Sionna's lips, even as Ruaidhri himself groaned in pain at the blow. Enraged, the Kilclares laid their hands upon their weapons, inducing a like response from the O'Neills. Like a Catherine wheel spitting sparks, Cullach's sword spun through his fingers, its well-whetted blade reflecting the flames of the firebrands as it twirled and came to rest upon Ruaidhri's nape. The threat was clear: If weapons were drawn, Ruaidhri would be the first to die. Sionna swallowed hard as she felt the prick of the O'Neill's *sgian-dubh* at her white throat. How had he slipped the dagger from his boot so quickly? Surely, he was a demon to be capable of such speed, such stealth—like an animal, she thought again, dismayed.

In the glade, no one moved, no one breathed. Only the drubbing of the rain, the rumble of the thunder, the roar of the sea, and the howling of the wind broke the stillness. Sionna's heart beat like the wings of a startled bird in her breast. Despite everything, she did not want to die in this clearing. But when the O'Neill spoke, his words belied at least that fear.

"If I am forced to slay your kinsman Ruaidhri ere you and I are wed, my lady, I will see to it that you nevertheless return with me to Ceann-Tìre," he grated, his topaz eyes boring into her sapphire ones, "although not, of course, as my bride—and that must prove a far less pleasant prospect than what you now face. For despite how you chafe against it, being my wife is preferable to being my whore, I'll warrant. Aye, you cannot deny that, my lady; for you are as proud as you are spirited, and even marriage to your lifelong foe is better than rape and disgrace at his hands—and those of his men—is it not? So, then, for your own sake, as well as Ruaidhri's, whatever the provocation, do not cry out again; do not help him to incite your clan to violence and bloodshed, and my own, also. Do you understand?"

"Aye, my lord." Sionna's voice was a strangled whisper.

That he would give her to his men for sport . . . He was heartless, monstrous, worse even than she had imagined. How could she wed him? Surely, even death was preferable! She had but to grab the bejeweled gold hilt of his *sgian-dubh*, to plunge the point deep into her throat . . .

"Nay, I'll not permit you to escape from me so easily as that, my lady," the O'Neill declared as he read her panicked intent in her wild eyes. Before she could act, he returned the dagger, with a smooth, deft flick of his wrist, to his boot. "Yours is a throat fashioned to receive a man's kisses, not the point of a blade. If you would be taught that lesson by me alone, then kneel, and let us proceed with the wedding ceremony ere the storm breaks upon us. Despite what you may think to the contrary, I am not so unsympathetic to your plight that I would have you spend your wedding night exposed to these wretched elements."

His hard, impassive visage gentled a trifle, much to Sionna's surprise and sudden confusion, for it was the first glimmer of hope she had that he was perhaps not as cruel as she feared. Slowly but obediently, she knelt upon the burgundy pillow before her.

"Kilclare"—the O'Neill's voice echoed challengingly in the glade—"do you give your daughter unto my keeping or nay?"

"Aye, I do." The reply was curt, grudging, acrimonious; but it was enough to cause those who had earlier laid hands upon their weapons to relax slightly. Glowering at Ruaidhri, the Kilclare strode grimly to the monolith to stand witness to the wedding ceremony that would render his only child as one dead to him and his clan forever.

There were few men who stood tall enough to look the Kilclare straight in the eye, but the O'Neill was one of them. For a long, taut moment, the two men stared at each other, each taking the other's measure, the Kilclare angered and aggrieved that his daughter should belong to a man such as this, the O'Neill arrogant and insolent as he glanced covetously at Sionna, then back at her father. The Kilclare's fists clenched tightly at his sides; with difficulty did he prevent himself from attacking his antagonist. As the O'Neill saw this, a sardonic smile curved his mouth, and intentionally, provocatively, he turned his back on the Kilclare, as though daring him to draw his *sgian-dubh* and to drive the dagger home.

Sionna's face whitened as she watched the hostile exchange; she gasped softly with shock and outrage as the O'Neill's gaze roamed over her so licentiously. Surely now, her father's steel would strike true and put an end to this mockery of a marriage! But it did not; and Sionna's heart sank as the O'Neill knelt beside her and, with a short nod, indicated to the nervously waiting priest to begin the wedding rite.

As the Latin words flowed over her, words she could not comprehend and to which she knew the responses only by rote, Sionna felt strangely as though she heard something more in the clearing, the low, melodious chanting of the ancient tribes, though it was surely no more than the drone of the rain and wind and sea. Yet as the sound murmured in her ears, it seemed somehow as though she were drawn beyond herself, back in time, back to this place; it seemed to be wreathed with smoke as well as mist, and dark, amorphous figures danced about the sacrificial fire—druids, shapeshifters, the animal skins that concealed their faces and bodies making them seem as unreal and unnerving as monsters from a nightmare. But she did not dream. That much only, Sionna knew with certainty when, as she and the O'Neill repeated their vows, his voice steady and sure, her own hushed and faltering, she felt the iciness and heaviness of the richly embellished band of old Celtic gold he slipped onto her finger, marking her for always as his. All else was a blur, aglow with a skein of torchlight and candlelight that wove like a dark red love knot about her and the man, the stranger, the enemy who was so soon become her husband. Deep then, Sionna drank from the silver chalice, bloodred wine that, for all its sweetness, tasted as bitter as poison upon her tongue. When at last the O'Neill lifted her face to his, she did not protest, but mutely obeyed his will.

His swarthy visage was now so close to hers that she could see her image reflected in the glittering depths of his tawny eyes. She could smell the sharp, grassy scent of vetiver that emanated from his skin, as fragrant as the forest and earth when it rained, and mingled with a subtler trace of musk. She could feel the warmth of his breath against her face. He was going to kiss her, she knew; for was that not what tradition dictated? Of their own volition, her lips parted; her tongue darted forth to moisten them, an unconsciously seductive gesture that caused the O'Neill's eyes to darken, to grow hungry with desire. His hands tangled roughly in the thick, heavy mass of her unbound hair; and with a low snarl, he crushed his mouth down upon hers, savagely sealing the troth they had plighted between them.

Sionna was unprepared for the ferocity of his kiss—hot, hard, demanding, silencing any outcry she might have made, shattering her stupored senses, and leaving her breathless in its wake. She had not known, had never dreamed that a kiss could be like this, as though a man were draining the very soul from her body and then pouring it back in. Her head reeled at the realization, at the hitherto unknown sensations he expertly stirred within her, frightening and perversely exciting her, making her feel as though she would swoon as his bold, insistent tongue ruthlessly compelled her resisting lips to open and insinuated itself inside, exultantly ravaging the moist sweetness within, leaving no part untasted, unsavored. Of their own accord, her hands twined about his neck as he bent her back slowly, inexorably, so she knew she would have fallen had he not held her so tightly, implacably molding her body against his own, making her intensely aware of him as a man—and one who wanted her. Shocked, scared, dazed by his desire and the magnitude of her own bewildering and terrifying emotions, Sionna tried belatedly to free herself from his captivating embrace, to no avail. She was his now, and he would not be denied. Only at her low moan of understanding and surrender did he finally release her, his eyes blazing with passion and triumph at what he had evoked in her—and with the promise of more yet to come.

For a timeless moment, the O'Neill stared down at her hungrily. Then, without warning, he swept her up into his strong arms and carried her to a bold black destrier brought forward by one of his men at his terse command. After settling Sionna firmly in the saddle, the O'Neill swung up behind her and, reaching around her, holding her close and secure, gathered the reins. Briefly, the huge, powerful horse fought the bit, snorting and rearing and prancing. But with an authoritative word and a decisive yank on the reins, the beast was brought to obey—and to stand before Ruaidhri, who glared up through red-misted eyes at the hated foe who had bested him and taken his betrothed.

"It is finished. Give over, be done of it," the O'Neill stated softly, coldly, his amber eyes merciless as he stared down at his hostage. "The woman is mine, and what is mine, I keep—and let no man take her away."

Ruaidhri's face mottled with fury at the contemptuous gibe. His eyes burned with animosity and pain.

"Damn you! I'll kill you, you bastard, you accursed demon! And take her beside you while your blood is yet warm!" he spat in return, making Sionna wince with hurt and dread at his brazen boast. Surely, he was as vicious and hubristic as she had always thought, that he should think not of her, but only of murder and revenge.

"My blood is warm tonight—and grows hotter all the while," the O'Neill shot back, his meaning unmistakable as he deliberately brushed his lips against Sionna's long black hair and laid one hand possessively upon her soft, trembling breast.

Then, laughing mockingly at Ruaidhri's impotent rage and torment, he set his spurs to his stallion's sides and bore his captive bride swiftly from the glade, headlong into the oncoming storm.

2

THEY had left the wooded vale behind and now galloped across the wild, sweeping moors along the cliffs that jutted over the beach far below. Pell-mell through the storm, they rode; for having simmered and boiled and rolled in rapidly from the eastern sea beyond, the tempest now unleashed its fury in full force upon them. Lightning shattered the firmament as though it were no more than a pane of fragile venetian glass, electrically charging the air so, the fine hairs on Sionna's nape stood on end, and she was sure that more than once, the earth itself was struck by the lethal bolts, burned and scorched—as the O'Neill's searing kiss had burned and scorched her. Thunder rumbled like the wheels of some giant, unearthly chariot racing across the roiling night sky, blacker than black with monstrous, madding clouds from which the rain sheeted down, tossed and blown by the wind that now, beyond the forest that had earlier checked its ferocity, had become a gale. Below, the sea rushed in upon the shivering sands to smash against the cliffs and to boom amid the natural stone arches to be found here and there along the coast. Jets of frothy spume rose high into the air, and spindrift flew upon the wind, tangy in Sionna's nostrils, salty upon her lips.

The O'Neill held her fast against him as they drove against the rain and wind, the powerful haunches of his destrier bunching and rippling beneath them with each mighty lunge across the boggy moors, the O'Neill using both whip and spurs to compel the steed on toward Ceann-Tìre in the distance. Even so, Sionna knew they could not possibly outrun the elements that blinded and battered them unmercifully; and she feared that at any moment, the horse would slip upon the marshy ground that, with each strong stride, sucked at its hammering hooves, so the animal did not so much gallop as leap forward. If the stallion should fall, its impetus would likely send her and the O'Neill tumbling over the crumbling edge of the cliffs, Sionna realized, terrified, to be broken upon their craggy, outcropping ledges and then the rocks that strewed the strand below. The beast's breath was labored, its shiny black coat sodden with rain, its deep chest lathered with foam that flew. Mud covered its belly and legs and spattered in clumps from its fiercely churning hooves. With the destrier's every onward plunge, the silver trappings of its bridle jangled loudly, mingling discordantly with the sharp, repeated crack of the O'Neill's lash.

For the first time that night, Sionna was glad of her husband's brutish strength and iron will that enabled him to retain control of the enormous steed and to force it on through the raging storm; for there was no place to take shelter upon the barren moors. Tight, she cleaved to the O'Neill, her face buried against his chest, the hood and folds of her cape drawn close about her to shield her as best they could from the weather. But the O'Neill himself sought no such protection. The cowl of his own sable cloak was thrown back, so his visage was fully bared. When she chanced to glance up at him, Sionna knew he welcomed his exposure to the elements. Upon his coarsely handsome countenance was an expression of intense exhilaration; his eyes gleamed with excitement at the challenge he faced, and once or twice, he actually laughed aloud, a deep, throaty sound that sent an icy grue up Sionna's spine and made her wonder uneasily if he was, in truth, mad. Yet she herself was not wholly immune to what gripped him—the wild, fearsome thrill born of the risk they were taking by pressing recklessly on to Ceann-Tire, the danger they courted by pitting themselves against nature's awesome forces.

"Hold tight, *cailin!*" the O'Neill shouted above the clamor of the savage storm. "We are almost home! There—at the end of the causeway—that is Ceann-Tire!"

As Sionna looked to where he pointed, her breath caught in her throat; for at that exact moment, a terrible, titanic trident of lightning split the heavens, and the fortress of which the O'Neill was lord and master was as suddenly revealed as though brought into existence by some evil necromancer's black magic. From the heart of an immense, rocky, sea-swept promontory connected by an ancient raised road to the mainland, the castle rose, cutting a stark, jagged silhouette against the night sky—dark, grim, and forbidding, soaring and scintillating like a monumental chunk of crystal shards possessed of some phenomenal, otherworldly power. Such was the eerie effect of the forked lightning, which, again and again, stabbed the daunting mass of flying turrets and looming towers, the imposing spiral of high, crenellated walls and lofty, machicolated battlements. Ceann-Tire. Land's End. The name was fitting, Sionna thought, shuddering, for she felt, in truth, that naught lay beyond the stronghold save the endless sea.

Slipping and sliding, they picked their way carefully along a steep, treacherous track that wended halfway down through the cliffs until it reached the head of the causeway. There, for the first time, the O'Neill's horse balked, rearing and prancing, whinnying and white-eyed with fear at what lay ahead—the long, narrow, cobbled stretch of raised road flanked by the turgid sea and awash with frothy waves. But the O'Neill had come too far to be thwarted now, and with lashing whip and roweling spurs, he propelled the animal forward. Its shod hooves clattered sharply on the cobblestones as it started reluctantly across the causeway, buffeted so by the rain and wind and sea that it seemed the stallion would be swept away at any moment—and the O'Neill and Sionna with it. Her heart lodged in her throat as she spied the cold, dark waves that, on either side of her, swirled and swelled and slammed against the causeway, spilling over its top to sluice upon the cobblestones, so it appeared as though the beast actually galloped across the very sea, its pounding hooves sending foam flying. She thought of drowning in the icy depths of that fathomless black water, and shivered and clutched the O'Neill even more tightly; and she did not care that when she again glanced up at him, instinctively seeking reassurance, his sensual mouth curved with amusement at how she clung to him and, like twin coals, his golden eyes glowed with exultation and desire. Whatever else Sionna had learned this night, foremost was that the O'Neill was like no other man she had ever known—shrewd, bold, daring, and powerful, bent on seizing life with a vengeance and bending it inexorably to his will. Deep down inside, she knew that thus would he bend her, also, in the end.

"Soon, my bride," the O'Neill muttered as he stared down at her white, upturned face pressed against his muscular chest. It was as though he had

read her mind, Sionna thought uneasily, trembling
violently against him, causing his grip upon her to
tighten painfully. Before she realized his intent, he
lowered his lips to hers and kissed her hard and
swiftly. "Very soon now, you shall be mine."

Perhaps it was no more than that they had at last
attained the end of the long causeway that made him
speak so to her, Sionna told herself resolutely, for it
filled her with misgiving to think the O'Neill could
guess her thoughts. Her mouth burned from his kiss;
she was angry and ashamed that it should feel so.
He was a stranger, her enemy . . . her husband.

Straining and creaking and groaning ominously
on its mammoth iron chains, the heavy wooden
drawbridge between the two U-shaped towers of the
gatehouse was slowly lowered to span the gap between causeway and castle; the iron-clad timber
portcullis was raised, and the two massive, iron-
bound wooden portals behind it were opened.
Ceann-Tìre was a stronghold in every sense of the
word, Sionna recognized with a sinking heart—un-
assailable, invulnerable, inescapable. The last, faint
ray of hope that she might yet find some means of
evading her fate died a cruel death.

The destrier thundered across the drawbridge and
beneath the gatehouse, whose supporting stone
walls formed a vaulted passage that was illuminated
by flickering torches set into iron sconces and that
gave way past a second portcullis and pair of doors
to the expansive outer ward. Beyond this lay a second high, circular wall and another gatehouse
whose equally secure set of barricades opened to reveal the smaller inner ward and the imposing keep
itself. As the O'Neill drew his steed to a halt and
dismounted, then lifted Sionna down from the saddle, a smattering of grooms hurried forward to greet
him and to take the exhausted horse in hand. Yet

though they clucked with dismay at the animal's snorting nostrils, frothy mouth, foamy chest, and heaving sides, they were careful to keep their distance from its teeth and hooves; and Sionna could have sworn she heard one of the men mumble, "Devil!" under his breath. She knew not if he referred to the stallion or to its master, for the bowing and scraping hostlers appeared to behold the O'Neill with as much dread as Sionna did.

Even more unnerving were the sly leers and looks of hatred she spied upon their faces as they eyed her covertly, some of them surreptitiously crossing themselves before leading the stallion away. But there was no time to dwell on the grooms' fear. Without warning, the O'Neill caught her up in his arms and, after treading swiftly up the short, wide flight of stone steps to the open doors of the donjon, carried her across the threshold into the great hall.

Sionna garnered only an impression of its vast size and once-opulent furnishings; for despite the fires that blazed in the four huge stone hearths, all was dark and dreary, smelling of must and mold, showing the unmistakable signs of neglect and decay, and eerily still. It was as though a pall lay over the castle, Sionna thought, disquieted, as though she had entered a place ancient and abandoned, where no human footstep had trodden in many a long year. At the realization that this was to be her new home, she shuddered in the O'Neill's arms; for that this should be her bridal welcome to Ceann-Tíre incensed and chagrined and utterly disheartened her. With difficulty, she fought back the sudden tears that stung her eyes.

To her fright and further discouragement, the O'Neill did not pause in the great hall, but, after issuing orders right and left to the handful of squires and servants who materialized to await his pleasure, bore her up a long, curving flight of stone stairs to the keep's private rooms. Down a drafty, narrow, seemingly interminable corridor lined with flaming iron cressets, he strode, then up a spiral stone staircase until he reached what were obviously his own apartments. Through the open doorway of the dismal antechamber, he conveyed her, and from there into a large tower that was as gloomy as all the rest. It was all Sionna could do to prevent her hot tears of wrath and humiliation from spilling over.

The fire that crackled in the stone hearth and the tarnished silver candelabra that dimly illuminated the bedchamber revealed that cobwebs laced the heavy, supporting beams of the high, vaulted ceiling and that dust balls lurked amid the worn fur rugs scattered upon the scarred oak floor. Moisture born of the storm seeped through the cold gray stone of which the tower was fashioned and dribbled in rivulets between the eroded seams of the ancient rocks. Water stains blotched the threadbare tapestries that hung upon the circular wall and that not only served as adornment, but also helped to keep out the bitter wind. Layers of dust swathed the dark, imposing furniture, dull and brittle from lack of polish, and clung to the folds of the heavy, faded, blue-velvet curtains suspended on rings from the intricately carved wooden canopy of the massive four-poster bed that dominated the room. North and south, twin pairs of stout, arched oak doors gave way onto balustraded balconies set deep into the ten-foot-thick tower wall. Flanking each of these apertures were two narrow, arched windows also deep-set into the tower wall and fitted with glass, iron grills, and shutters. Musty draperies matching those on the bed hung at each window well, each of which had built-in storage benches topped with mice-eaten cushions.

"Welcome to Ceann-Tìre, *mo bean-bainnse,*" the

O'Neill uttered huskily as he set Sionna in the center of the room, making no apology for its deteriorated state. For a long moment, he stared down at her intently, his hands on her arms, holding her prisoner. Then he slowly pushed her ermine-trimmed hood back from her arresting face and began deliberately to unfasten the heavy gold brooch that pinned her sable mantle, as though daring her to protest his intimate, possessive action. "By the saints, you are a braw *cailin*, a fit mate for me, in truth; for any other woman would have fainted in my arms during that hellish ride. I marvel you did not."

Slipping her dripping cloak from her shoulders, he allowed it to fall to the floor, uncovering her exquisite wedding gown fashioned of costly midnight-blue silk, which, now soaked from the rain, clung revealingly to her slender, voluptuous figure. Inhaling sharply, the O'Neill feasted upon the sight, as though she were a slave upon a block and he a prospective buyer, while Sionna flushed and cast down her eyes, biting her lower lip hard to still its sudden trembling and wishing she were not so very beautiful, so finely and seductively arrayed. Only her mother's tearful entreaty to be wise and not to enrage the O'Neill from the beginning had persuaded her to don the dress earlier this morning, when she would much rather have clothed herself in mourning, in sackcloth and ashes, instead. Now, Sionna heartily wished she had followed her own inclination, for she felt abruptly and horribly as though she stood stark naked before the O'Neill, vulnerable to his every desire and command.

The dress's low-cut bodice exposed generously the soft white swell of her full, round breasts, which rose and fell rapidly, enticingly, with her every ragged breath. Its long, snug sleeves gradually widened at the wrists to trail in graceful, elongated triangles to the floor, so that when she moved, she seemed to glide as ethereally as a goddess, as regally as a queen. From its narrow waist and hips—the latter encircled by a fine-linked gold girdle that bore her small, bejeweled dinner knife—the gown swept in elegant folds to the floor, its hem flowing into an extravagant train at the back. Bordered all around with gold trim, the dress was complemented by a long, sleeveless gold surcoat, soft slippers, and, at her ears, throat, and wrists, gold Celtic jewelry set with brilliant sapphires that reflected the midnight-blue of her eyes. Her long hair—as black and gleaming as obsidian; unbound, as tradition dictated for a bride; and interwoven with small, intricate braids twined with gold ribands—cascaded in soft, rain-dampened waves to her knees.

Her entire appearance was designed to please a man; and from beneath the veil of her lashes, Sionna saw by the glint in his topaz eyes that its effect upon the O'Neill was undeniably potent. Her mother would have counseled her to use the O'Neill's obvious lust for her to soften and to seduce him to her will; but this Sionna, young and proud and afraid of what he had already stirred to life inside her, could not bring herself to do. He was not a man to be ruled by a woman, she thought, but, rather, one who would take what he wanted, whether she wished it or not, and undeceived by any guile on her part.

Yet when he made no immediate move to fall upon her and ravish her, she dared to toss her head disdainfully at her drab surroundings, to turn away from him, to go and warm herself before the fire. It was as she stretched out her hands to the blaze that Sionna noticed the large portrait mounted above the hearth, its ornate, gilded frame draped with cobwebs, the painting itself dark and shadowed, dull with dust and crazed with time. Yet still did she recognize the woman in the picture, and she gasped audibly with shock, bewildered, for it was her own image that stared back at her from the portrait!

"Aye, so did I feel when I first beheld you tonight in the forest," the O'Neill murmured as he came to stand beside her, his tawny eyes aglow with a fierce, peculiar light, "for though I had heard stories of your uncommon beauty, it was not until then that I was certain you were the one. The painting was done from an old, crude sketch; still, the resemblance is striking, is it not? It might be you, in truth, *mo bean-bainnse.*"

"Are you saying that 'tis not?" Sionna inquired, puzzled, her eyes searching his intently.

"Aye—"

"But, then . . . who, my lord?"

"Can you not guess, *cailin?* 'Tis the woman—the witch—Igrania of Clare Caiseal, who did lay her curse upon the Clan O'Neill of Clandeboye. She was burned at the stake—at the very heart of the standing stones where you and I were married tonight. 'Tis why I chose it as our meeting place. 'Tis why I chose *you*, my lady. You are directly descended from the sorceress Igrania, her blood strong and undiluted in your veins."

"My lord!" Sionna cried softly at this revelation. "I know naught of the curse said to afflict your clan and certainly possess no magic to rescind it! I am no witch, no sorceress, I promise you! If that was your reason for wedding me, you have profited as little as I. That being so, will you not let me go, my lord?" she implored earnestly. "Our marriage can yet be annulled . . ."

"Nay, *mo bean-bainnse.*" Despite his great disappointment that she did not know how to lift the curse that lay upon him, the O'Neill kept his voice low and determined, as smooth as honey in Sionna's ears, making her tremble as she thought once more of how his kiss had burned her. "I'll not release you, not ever—for witch or nay, you have bewitched me, in truth. For that alone will I keep you, so speak no more of regaining your freedom. Your place now is here at Ceann-Tìre—at my side and in my bed—and there is an end to it, my lady!"

He spoke no more, nor did she; for now, his squires and servants appeared, bearing, to Sionna's surprise, buckets of steaming-hot water with which to fill the hammered-brass bathtub that sat to one side of the hearth, soft towels and sponges, and scented soaps, oils, powders, and perfumes. They also carried platters and bowls laden high with food, and pitchers brimming with ale and mulled wine. Wet, hungry, and weary to the bone, Sionna felt an unexpected rush of gratitude toward the O'Neill, and it was with difficulty that she bit back the impulsive words of thanks that sprang to her lips. She owed him not even so much as that, she told herself fiercely. He was her enemy, and she, his captive.

A cloth was laid upon the side table that stood against the wall, and the cold but ample repast spread upon it. The bathtub, drawn forth and placed before the hearth, was filled nigh to overflowing, the water softened with fragrant oils. Then the squires and menservants gathered all but a few of the remaining pails of water, intended for rinsing, to haul them into the antechamber, while the serving maids moved silently to begin divesting Sionna of her wedding costume and to undo the braids in her hair. She swallowed hard at the thought that the O'Neill meant to stay and watch her toilette; it was his right as her husband, after all. But to her relief, he announced peremptorily that she had half an hour to make ready. Then, closing the door behind him, he followed the squires and menservants to the antechamber, where his own bath was being prepared.

It would have helped, Sionna knew, had the serving maids been her own, chattering and teasing and laughing to ease what was more than just maidenly apprehension of her wedding night. But they were not. When they spoke to her at all, it was sullenly, with all the contempt they felt toward the Clan Kilclare; and they eyed her with the same sly knowing and loathing she had spied upon the faces of the grooms—and believed she understood now, since seeing Igrania's portrait. So marked was Sionna's resemblance to her ancestor that it must seem as though Igrania herself had returned to Ceann-Tìre—and would this night receive her just desserts in the arms of the O'Neill.

Once Sionna was naked, the women examined her flawless body from head to toe, searching, she knew, for the telltale mark of a witch. But she was without blemish, scar, or deformity, much to her relief; for she felt that if any of these had been found upon her, the serving maids would not have hesitated to denounce her and to insist that, like Igrania, she, too, be burned at the stake. She wondered if the O'Neill would have permitted her to die in such a hideous manner; she wondered, horrified, how many other Kilclare women had suffered such a fate in this grim and dour household.

Though Sionna refused to gratify them by voicing an objection, the women soaped and scrubbed too roughly both her lustrous black hair and her lissome white body, then rinsed her off and vigorously toweled her dry. Then, in a process that was like some pagan ritual, Sionna thought, troubled, as though they prepared her to be sacrificed instead of mated, they powdered and perfumed her until her skin gleamed with the soft sheen of a pearl. The fragrance the serving maids used was unfamiliar to her—

strong, wild, and musky, with a faint trace of vetiver, like the scent of some feral animal mingled with
that of grass and forest. It seemed to permeate her
skin, both disturbing and exciting her. She yearned
to wash it off; but already, the women were attiring
her in a gossamer white night rail and a matching
wrapper, both of which did little to conceal her
charms.

"But—but . . . these aren't mine," Sionna protested as she gazed down at the apparel, so shock-
ingly sheer and clinging that her nipples and
womanhood showed alluringly through the soft,
sensuous material. "Where are my coffers? Where
are my own garments?" she asked sharply, trying to
quell her abruptly rising hysteria; for a wagon
loaded with her wedding trousseau and other per-
sonal possessions had accompanied her and her
father's men from Clare Caiseal. Did the O'Neill
mean, then, to deny her even her own belongings?
Did he mean to keep her virtually naked and imprisoned in this tower?

"No man save his lordship be mad enough to ride
through this storm, my lady," one of the serving
maids replied coolly, scornfully, as though this
should be obvious to anyone. "Those who accompanied him will have sought shelter in the woods
until morn, when they will return home, doubtless
bringing your coffers with them if the moors be dry
enough for the wagon to pass. Until then, his lordship has bidden you to wear what has been
provided."

Sionna felt like a fool at the woman's words. Of
course, the O'Neills had taken refuge in the forest;
of course, a heavily burdened vehicle could not tra-
verse the miry moors on a night such as this. Even
now, as the women sat her on a low stool before the
fire, spreading her long black hair to dry and brush-

ing it until it gleamed like jet, Sionna could hear the
rain beating against the unshuttered windows and
upon the conical slate roof of the tower, and the
wind whining through the narrow passages of the
donjon. Forcing herself to take deep breaths, she attempted to calm herself, not wanting the serving
maids to guess how tautly strung her nerves were,
how close she felt to some fine edge that separated
sanity from madness.

Moments later, his own ablutions completed, the
O'Neill appeared in the doorway, garbed now in a
flowing white shirt that displayed a goodly portion
of his powerful chest heavily matted with dark hair,
a leather belt slung about his hips, and a pair of tight
black chausses that left little to the imagination
where his potent masculinity was concerned. Sionna
caught her breath sharply at the sight of him; coloring with mortification, she quickly averted her
gaze—though not before she glimpsed his own
covetous appraisal of her, the desire that flared in
his eyes, the slow, sensual smile that curved his lips.
He was so huge that he would surely split her in
twain! She was so horrified by the thought that it
was not until the O'Neill came to stand before her
that she realized they were alone now, that having
emptied the bathtub and collected the damp towels,
the toiletries, and her wedding finery, the serving
maids had departed, shutting the door behind them.

"I am famished, as you must be also, and I would
dine, my lady." The O'Neill indicated the laden side
table.

When Sionna did not move, he lifted one devilish
brow, glancing at her expectantly, and with a start,
she realized he intended her to serve him. Though
she was tempted to refuse, the fear of provoking him
now that they were alone together urged her instead
to comply with his silent demand. Wordlessly, she

rose, intensely aware of her nakedness beneath the diaphanous robe and night rail that were all that stood between her and him, and acutely cognizant of how his eyes devoured her.

"Will you—will you have wine or ale, my lord?" she asked.

"Wine, *cailin.*"

Blushing deeply with fury and shame that she should be so scantily clad and defenseless before him, Sionna tried unsuccessfully with one hand to keep the wrapper drawn close about her as she poured a goblet of wine and prepared a trencher of the cold meats and cheeses and dried fruit arrayed upon the platters. But in the end, she needed both hands to carry the cup and the hollowed-out loaf of bread filled with food; and when she knelt beside the O'Neill on the fur rug upon which he now lounged before the blazing hearth, her robe gaped to reveal the low-cut nightgown, exposing her breasts, her rosy nipples rigid with fear and cold and some other inexplicable emotion she could not name. She heard the hiss of his sharply indrawn breath; and with shaking hands, she gingerly set the repast upon the stool she had sat on earlier, then, clutching the edges of the wrapper together convulsively, quickly turned without permission to fetch her own meal.

"Nay." The O'Neill's hand shot out swiftly, catching her wrist and pulling her back down beside him, his breath labored. After a tense moment, a muscle flexing in his jaw, he said, "We will share the bridal feast, as is customary, *mo bean-bainnse.*" Picking up the heavy silver goblet, he took a liberal swallow of the rich, dark red wine. Then, handing the cup to Sionna, he commanded, "Drink. 'Twill help to soothe you."

Though she abhorred the intimacy of sharing one

goblet, one trencher, she drank obediently, long and deep. She was careful to turn the cup so her mouth did not touch the place where his own had rested— something that did not escape his notice. The corners of his lips lifted in a sarcastic smile that did not quite reach his narrowed eyes, which glittered with anger at the insult.

"So, my lady, like a spirited mare, you do yet chafe at the unaccustomed bit between your teeth," he observed softly, in a way that made Sionna wonder why she had dared yet again to rebel against him and caused the pulse at the base of her throat to flutter wildly. "You do yet shy away from the touch of your master. But you resist in vain, *mo bean-bainnse*, for I *will* tame you. Aye, ere this night is ended, I shall be in your saddle, and you shall be glad 'tis I who rides you, I swear!"

Sionna gasped with outrage at his crude, conceited boast.

"Art so arrogant as that, then? Art mad, in truth!" she cried, shaking, aghast and unable to choke back the hot, impulsive words that tumbled from her lips. "Nay, a thousand times nay, I would refuse you if given a choice! I do not want you! Did you think that 'twould be otherwise when 'twas unwillingly I wed you, as well you know? You are a stranger to me, my mortal foe—"

"Nay, I am your husband, your lord and master, as well *you* know, *cailin*. Did you think I would not claim what is mine?" he questioned sharply. "Nay, you knew full well the consequences of the bargain made, that I was unlikely to have demanded you as the price for Ruaidhri's life and freedom if I did not want you as my bride—and in my bed. What man would not? Your beauty is legend, the subject of bard song; it stirs the blood and quickens the loins. Well now can I understand Ruaidhri's obvious obsession with you."

Ruaidhri! Sionna had not thought of him since leaving the wooded glen behind. Had she loved him, her conscience would have pricked her sorely for that. But she had not. Still, she felt honor-bound to inquire after his welfare.

"And did you keep your share of the bargain, my lord?" she queried stiffly. "Or does Ruaidhri even now lie in his grave?"

"What do you care, *mo bean-bainnse*? Upon hearing Cullach's words in your father's great hall, did you not cry out that you did not love Ruaidhri, that he could rot in my dungeons or rot in hell, for all you cared? Aye, you did, for so Cullach told me. Nor was it love and anguish at your forced parting from Ruaidhri that I spied upon your face when my men dragged him forth into the clearing. Rather, 'twas anger that his stupidity had compelled you to become *my* bride instead of his.

"In your mind, I was, of course, the greater of two evils—though he would have used you far more ill than I will, I promise you. Nay, do not bother to dispute it, for I know that you don't believe it—and in truth, why should you? By your own admission, you are innocent and so can know naught of how a man's character shapes his manner in bed—or do you now say that you played me false at the standing stones, my lady?" The O'Neill paused for a moment, permitting the silence to grow heavy between them. When Sionna did not answer, he gave a low, mocking laugh. "Nay, I thought not. For all your bold spirit, you blush too easily to be aught but chaste, *cailin*, and your maidenly fear of me is evident.

"But to answer your question: Aye, my men had orders to release Ruaidhri once you and I were safe across the moors. He does spend this night alive and free—though no less miserable, I'll warrant, than he was in the dungeons of Ceann-Tìre. Doubtless even now, he drinks himself into a stupor and bewails his privation to any and all who will listen; for fool, indeed, is Ruaidhri—and more fool for having lost you. I am not so careless. What I take, I hold. You belong to me, *mo bean-bainnse*—and I *shall* have what is mine. Do you doubt it?"

"Perhaps not, my lord"—Sionna's voice quavered slightly and held a bitter, contemptuous note—"for you are much stronger than I, and rape has long been a man's way of proving his dominance over a woman."

"Aye, but 'twill be far more pleasurable for us both if it does not come to that." Withdrawing his dinner dagger from his leather belt, the O'Neill cut a piece of roast venison from the portion in the trencher and, after stabbing and consuming the morsel, swallowed it down with more of the wine. "You are my wife and not entitled to refuse me; but for all that you may believe otherwise, I do think to spare you pain."

"Then it *does* hurt!—the coupling . . . " she exclaimed softly, quailing at the knowledge; for though her mother had warned her as much, Sionna had at the time been so stunned and emotionally wrought by her wretched fate that the words had not registered—only that no matter what was demanded of her, however shocking or shameful, she must submit, must not fail to please the O'Neill, her lord and master.

"Aye," he replied tersely, "for a maid, the first time—and often ever after, if she is broken hard, without being properly readied."

"Readied? I—I—" Sionna broke off abruptly, biting her lower lip and reddening at her ignorance. As beasts coupled, so a man mounted a woman and took her—and the act was painful. What more was there to know? "I—I don't understand, my lord."

"Nay, but *I* do, *mo bean-bainnse*—and that is enough for us both if only you do not choose to fight me."

The O'Neill spoke no more then, allowing her to digest not only his words, but also the food he proffered her—chunks of the venison, mutton, and game birds, all cooked so much rarer than to what she was accustomed that Sionna marveled he did not send to the kitchen to chide the cook for how underdone the meat was. Picking and choosing, skewering with his dinner dagger what pleased him, he handed her pieces of the cheeses, bits of the dried fruit, and slices of the bread, which he spread generously with butter. She washed down the meal with the wine he insisted she drink, even when she attempted to refuse it, feeling herself, already tired, growing muddled and even more drowsy from the potent alcohol. Soon, it began to seem she but dreamed the storm outside and the fire within and the O'Neill himself at her side.

Surely, it *must* be a dream; for all the while he fed her, he kissed and caressed her—and she did nothing to deter him. He touched her so lightly and quickly that each time when she would have protested, it was too late. He was already offering her another bite of food, another sip of wine, confusing and unsettling her because she did not understand why he did not simply ravish her and be done with it, why he should torture her in this terrible fashion, prolonging her agonized suspense. Unwisely, in an effort to calm herself, to bolster her flagging courage, she had drunk far too much of the wine he continued to press upon her. Her mind was beclouded and benumbed; yet, perversely, her body felt as though it were a mass of heady sensation—vibrant, quivering, teeming with life. The O'Neill's every slightest touch upon her skin was excruciating, unbearable.

Aye, 'twas the wine. It *must* be the wine, she told herself, that made her feel as though her senses were scattered to the winds and that caused her to flush and to perspire as though she sat too near the fire.

But in some dark cranny of her mind, Sionna knew that with each kiss, each caress, the O'Neill somehow heightened the giddiness and lassitude that assailed her and that this was his deliberate intent. Even so, she did not know how to make him stop, felt hopelessly mixed up and weak when he kissed and stroked her black hair, her dusky cheek, her white skin, slowly accustoming her to the feel of his lips and hands upon her. With his thumbs, he traced tiny circles upon her eyelids, her cheeks, her mouth, and tugged gently at her moist lower lip, causing her to tremble with longings she could not name. With his tongue, he outlined her mouth before kissing her tenderly, fleetingly, leaving her yearning curiously, despite herself, for the hardness, the hunger with which he had kissed her at the heart of the standing stones and at the end of the storm-swept causeway. She was scarcely even aware of how he adroitly eased the robe from her body, felt only how he pressed his lips to the sensitive place where her shoulder joined her nape and how, with his tongue, he teased her there, making her whimper and shudder at the sudden, fierce tremor that shot through her. His palms glided down to cup her breasts; through the thin fabric of her night rail, he rotated his thumbs languorously across her roseate nipples, causing them to contract and to stiffen and to send queer tingles through her entire body. With the merest brush of his fingers, he freed her burgeoning breasts from their flimsy constraints and, lowering his mouth to her nipples, sucked them and laved them greedily with his tongue. Unwittingly,

Sionna moaned low in her throat at the fervent feelings he stirred within her, feelings that were like the electric portents that presaged a gathering storm.

At the sound, the O'Neill lifted his head; his hands slid up to ensnare the tresses at her temples, turning her face up to his. For an eternity, it seemed, he gazed down at her, his amber eyes burning with a dark and dangerous desire. Then, without warning, his mouth swooped down to seize possession of her own, his tongue plunging between her lips, compelling them to part; and Sionna understood, abruptly terrified, that at last, her time of waiting had come to an end.

He kissed her as no other man had ever kissed her, at once frightening and igniting within her the incomprehensible, wild, leaping flame he had somehow kindled earlier in the glade and that now seemed, incredibly, to blaze even hotter and brighter than before. As flushed and faint as though suddenly ailing with fever, she swayed on her knees; of their own volition, her hands crept up to press against the O'Neill's chest, steadying her. Gasping, she tried instinctively to turn her head away, to free herself from his grasp. But his strong hands held her prisoner, and she could not escape. In moments, she would be his. She was stricken to the heart by the realization. That she should be conquered so easily angered and frightened and shamed her. Where was her pride, her honor? He was her enemy; centuries of feuding lay between her clan and his. Was she a wanton or mad that she should yield to him so compliantly, without a struggle? Their marriage was a mockery; he had no right to touch her! How much sweeter, then, the taste of his triumph would be if she willingly submitted to him, disgracing herself and betraying Ruaidhri and her clan. She would not; she *could* not!

"Don't, my lord," she breathed against his relent-
lessly encroaching lips, striving desperately to fight
the waves of light-headedness and lethargy in which
she felt herself drowning, to fight him, who was her
nemesis. "Please don't."

"Don't what, *mo bean-bainnse*?" The O'Neill's voice
was low, thick, his breath torrid against her sultry
skin as his lips scalded their way urgently across her
fair cheek to her temple, her hair. Ardently, he
rained kisses upon the ebony tresses, tangled his
hands in the soft, silken strands. "Don't kiss you?
Don't touch you? *Ach, cailin.* You might as well ask
me to fetch down the moon from the night sky.
'Twould be an easier task than my keeping my
mouth and hands from you, I swear. So, hush,
now—and let me have my will of you. Let me teach
you what I would have you learn."

Though the smoothly spoken words were soft and
loverlike, they were only intended to deceive her,
Sionna knew. The O'Neill had no love for her; he
only wanted her. To him, she was nothing more than
a captive bride he had demanded out of enmity and
revenge, constraining her to wed him in exchange
for Ruaidhri's life and freedom. What a master of
seduction, a demon, in truth, the O'Neill was, insid-
iously tempting her into his dark realm of smoke
and fire, where he would dishonor her and use her
as carelessly as he would have used a whore. Young,
proud, and afraid, spurred by these thoughts that
drove like the sharp spikes of a mace into her dulled
brain, Sionna now twisted and turned like a
wounded wild animal in his embrace, seeking fran-
tically to elude him; and when she could not, she
clawed blindly at his handsome visage, leaving
deep, vicious gouges.

"Damn you, witch!" the O'Neill grated when he
touched his fingers to his injured cheek and saw that

they came away streaked with blood. "Faith! So, this is how you would repay my patience and consideration, is it, by God?"

His golden eyes narrowed at the affront, gleaming dark with wrath and passion as they bored into Sionna's ashen countenance, her blue eyes wide with terror at her own temerity and the recognition of how she had enraged him. She cringed and cried out softly when, in retaliation, he abruptly delivered a stinging, backhanded slap to her face, sending her sprawling headlong upon the fur rug. Stunned and gasping, she lay there shivering, waiting for the much harder blows that would surely follow. But instead of beating her, as she had fully expected, the O'Neill swept her up into his arms and, striding swiftly to the bed, flung her down roughly, his visage hard with determination as he stared down at her, wounded and angry—and wanting her now more than ever.

Behind him, beyond the rain-blurred windows, lightning violently cracked apart the night sky and thunder bellowed as, with a single, rapid movement, he yanked off his shirt to reveal his massive, hirsute chest and heavily muscled arms, an expanse of bare bronze flesh as smooth and sheeny as though fragrant oil had been poured into his bathwater, also. To Sionna's stricken eyes, he resembled some pagan god, towering over her, his merciless gaze pinning her to the mattress, grimly daring her to move and threatening her with dire consequences if she did. But when his hands fell to his leather belt and began to unbuckle it, she thought, horrified, that he intended to thrash her with it; and at that, impelled by fear, her head spinning at the effort, she did half rise and try to flee.

As quick as a predator springing, with a low snarl, the O'Neill caught her long hair and jerked her back;

and when he sank beside her on the bed, she saw that he was now utterly naked, his big, bold shaft hard and heavy with desire, and she knew then how he intended to punish her. Summoning her last ounce of strength, she strove mightily against him in a final, desperate attempt to combat him, her nails raking his chest as she grappled with him furiously—in vain. For what was her strength compared to his? He had made that clear to her from the start, had he not? His hands ruthlessly forced her down, then easily grabbed her wrists tight and pinioned them securely above her head as, throwing one leg across her body to restrain her yet further, he purposely leaned his weight upon her, expelling all the air from her lungs and constraining her to lie still so she could breathe. Gasping, whimpering, faint and fatigued by her futile contention, Sionna ceased to struggle; and after that, her wispy nightgown was but a poor deterrent to his lust, brutally torn from her shrinking body and impatiently cast aside to expose her fully to his salacious scrutiny.

The O'Neill inhaled sharply as the fire and candlelight danced across her pale, glowing skin, illuminating the rosy crests of her soft white breasts and casting shadows upon the ebony nest between her trembling thighs. She was even more beautiful than he had imagined—and she was his . . . His loins tightened keenly at the knowledge. His breath coming in hard rasps, he slowly, deliberately, trailed his hand down over her breasts to her shuddering belly, then lower still, to the silken curls that concealed the secret heart of her. Then, his palm resting lightly there, where no other man had ever touched her, his tawny eyes intent upon her dazed, frightened face, he spoke softly—though no less resolutely.

"Now then, *cailin*, you have had a lesson in the two ways a man can take a woman—gentle or rough. For though there are a hundred others, they are but variations, and you will learn those, too, in time, in this bed, *my* bed, *mo bean-bainnse*; for I am a man who likes it all ways with a woman—and shall like it even more so with you." His eyes roamed over her in a way that left her no room to doubt his words. "Still, though you have tried my patience sorely and there are just as many pleasures to be had from a rough tumble, as I shall also teach you, 'tis gently I would yet take you this first time. So, now, I ask you—and mark me well, my lady: I shall not be asking a second time—will you yield to me or nay?"

His unflinching gaze riveted her where she lay; and of a sudden, Sionna knew she did not want him callously to beat and to rape her, as she feared he was capable of doing.

"Aye, my lord, I yield," she whispered brokenly, defeated. She was too dizzy, too frail, too exhausted to try yet again to escape from him, to go on contesting him, especially when she knew with certainty that neither would avail her aught in the end. For even if she gained her liberty, where would she go? And even if by some miracle she managed to stave him off, there would be other nights. Sooner or later, he would prevail. "I yield ... "

"Then put your arms around my neck and kiss me, *cailin*," he demanded huskily as he slowly released her, his eyes softening, darkening with desire and jubilant satisfaction at her response.

For a moment, Sionna hesitated, swallowing hard, her heart pounding at his lustful glance, his carnal mouth so close to her own. Then, finally, as though she were entranced, her hands crept up his broad chest to twine about his neck, and she pressed her lips tentatively to his. After that, it seemed she lost the power to think, the will to oppose him, became mindless, shapeless, all her bones dissolving inside her. Fluid, flowing, she could only feel and acquiesce and respond as he returned her kiss, his mouth moving gently upon hers at first, then gradually growing hungrier, more insistent, his tongue shooting deep between her lips, twisting, teasing, tantalizing, making her breath catch in her throat and filling her with fear and insidious excitement. She felt as she had riding through the unbridled storm—wild and exhilarated. It seemed as he bent over her, kissing and stroking her as he had earlier, that the O'Neill *was* the storm, crumbling the last vestiges of her resistance as surely as the rain and wind and sea eroded the cliffs that edged the shore. His mouth and tongue and hands seemed to be everywhere upon her now, tasting and touching, kissing and caressing, more potent and intoxicating than the rich, dark red wine Sionna had drunk at the heart of the standing stones and before the fire that burned in the tower hearth—as a fire burned in her, expertly fed and stoked by the man who held her in his embrace.

Sweat from its heat dampened her hair, glistened on her fair skin. With agonizing slowness, he licked away the moisture that trickled down the valley between her breasts. Aching with passion, her breasts themselves swelled eagerly to fill his cupped palms, her nipples as hard as taut buds bursting to unfold their dusky-pink petals. Deeply, the O'Neill inhaled their wild, musky fragrance, sucked the heady nectar of her breasts as though to imprint both scent and taste upon his memory, so he would be drawn to it always, like a bee to one special pollen. Of their own accord did the petals open, and sweet was the sting of his questing tongue before his winged lips took flight to light upon her mouth again, her tresses that, like slender, trailing vines, entangled and garlanded them, binding them together.

"Sionna . . . " he muttered hoarsely against her throat. "Sweet Sionna . . . how I want you! See how I desire you? Touch me, taste me . . . yes . . . ah, yes, *mo bean-bainnse* . . . "

The black hair that matted his chest was like a velvet thicket against her fingertips and breasts, in sharp contrast to the muscles, as hard as horn, that rippled and quivered beneath her palms when she explored him, marveling at his handsomeness, his strength. He was without equal; instinctively, she had known that from the beginning, when she had first beheld him in the glade—bold, barbarous, no ordinary man, but something more, something that, although he was her enemy, had drawn her to him despite herself. It drew her helplessly now. His sweat-dampened flesh gleamed like burnished bronze in the firelight; the tang of salt met her mouth and tongue when she kissed him, tasted him, touching him everywhere she could reach, discovering him as he discovered her, with pleasure and passion that spiraled ever upward, ever stronger as Sionna lost awareness of time's passing, lost awareness of anything save him and the exquisite embers of emotion he fanned to flame within her.

Then, at last, the O'Neill spread her thighs wide to stroke the soft, engorged nether lips that cleaved at his touch. Lightly did his finger slip deep into the moist, dark heart of her, only to withdraw tortuously before thrusting in again and yet again, joined by a second finger to stretch her even farther, heightening her readiness to receive him. Sionna gasped and shuddered at the intimacy of the caress and involuntarily arched against him, whimpering. He kissed her mouth to still her, his tongue mimicking the sweetly agonizing movements of his hand as he fondled her, his thumb rubbing the quivering nub that was the key to her pleasure. With each plunge

of his fingers, each flick of his thumb, her desire for
him grew until she ached with a terrible, unendur-
able hollowness at the liquid core of her, yearned
fervidly to be filled by him. Thrashing her head and
moaning, driven by blind, primitive need for him,
she writhed and bucked against him, his quick stroking no longer enough to satisfy; and he knew she
was nearing her peak, was ready, craving for him to
mount her.

"My lord ... please," she sobbed, not knowing
what it was she strained toward, only that she felt
she must attain it or die.

"I have a name, Sionna. Say it, damn you!" he
rasped against her lips, the hand he had snarled in
her disheveled hair tightening, jerking her head back
so he could see her face. "Tell me that you want
me—and me alone!"

"Aye, Lucan ... I do. I want you ... only you.
Please ... take me, Lucan! Take me now ... " she
begged shamelessly.

He needed no further urging. On corded arms, he
rose, poising himself above her, his long, shaggy
black hair falling about his shoulders, his saturnine
features alternately illuminated, then cast into
shadow by the flickering fire, making him appear
suddenly, eerily, like some half man, half beast as he
bent over her, dark and swarthy and naked, sheened
with sweat and fragrant with musk. His amber eyes
glowed intensely with hunger and exultation as he
stared down at her. There was between them a moment as highly charged as the storm that raged beyond the tower. Then, abruptly, he took her,
penetrating her deeply in a blinding moment of
white-hot pain that was all invading, all conquering,
an absolute incursion that demanded her total submission. At the shock of his entry and the severing of
her fragile maidenhead, Sionna cried out, a low wail

of surrender that the O'Neill swallowed with his triumphant lips, kissing and stroking her, and murmuring soothingly that the pain would pass. For a time, he lay still atop her, accustoming her to the feel of him inside her. Then, after slowly withdrawing, he entered her again, more gently now that her virtue no longer barred his path. Then, gradually, he began to move within her, his hands beneath her hips, lifting her to meet each thrust, teaching her the rhythm. Soon, Sionna found that the pain did indeed dissipate, as he had promised, to be replaced by pleasure as, no longer able to restrain himself, the O'Neill drove ever harder and deeper and faster into her, his head buried against her shoulder, his breath hot and harsh against her skin. Then, at last, his body quickened feverishly against her own, and she clung to him wantonly as the storm outside seemed suddenly to roar in her ears, as though she were once more exposed to the full force of its fury, the wind rising, the rain drumming, the sea churning until all the elements came together in a massive surge of tempestuous power that swept her up and bore her aloft, hurtling her into a swirling black maelstrom that suddenly exploded in a brilliant burst of lightning that was blinding, bedazzling, breathtaking, burning her to cinders before evanescing into darkness and silence. Against her, the O'Neill groaned and shuddered long and hard as he spilled his seed inside her. Then he collapsed atop her, panting, his heart beating in frantic unison with her own as they lay still together in the quiet afterglow of their lovemaking.

After a time, he withdrew, kissing her tenderly and cradling her against his chest, his warm embrace both possessive and yet curiously comforting. For now that it was over, Sionna wept bitterly in his arms, awed and frightened and confused by what had erupted between them, like the storm through which they had galloped. Except that this time, he had ridden her, coaxing and urging her to a fiery passion that had in the end overwhelmed and utterly consumed her. She was ashamed at how easily and thoroughly he had conquered her, how she had begged him, her enemy, to take her. Now, what just moments past had felt so wild and glorious seemed base and degrading. She throbbed at the secret heart of her, swollen and sore from his painful entry. Between her thighs, she felt the warmth of her virgin's blood, mingled with his seed; on her flesh, she smelled the musky fragrance of their primal mating.

He was like an animal, Sionna thought, dismayed, and some dark, earthy thing inside her own self had responded to him on that primitive level, had wanted him—as she would not have wanted him, would never have wanted him if he had beaten and raped her. With his patience, his knowledge, and his skill, he had wakened her desire and sated it, showing her the pleasures to be had from the act and knowing that only he, her husband, had the right to lie with her; and if she would find such ecstasy again, she must seek it in his arms—and his alone. What a terrible weapon she had unwittingly permitted him to gain against her, Sionna realized, stricken, and how well and ruthlessly would he wield it! For she did not doubt that he would take her again, countless times again, forcing her to respond, bedeviling and enslaving her . . .

As though he had read her mind, the O'Neill's arms abruptly tightened around her, his manhood stirred once more by her nearness, her nakedness. The scent of her, of their mating, permeated his nostrils, arousing and intoxicating him. Wrapping his hands in her tousled tresses, he tilted her face up to his to claim her mouth deeply again, his tongue tasting the tears that stained her lips and compelling her tremulous lips to open, to yield to him.

" 'Tis done, *mo bean-bainnse*," he muttered. "You are mine now, only mine, forever mine. Why, then, do you seek to resist me? You are a virgin no longer. So what does it matter how many times I have you?"

"It matters, my lord!" she answered softly, fiercely. "It matters!"

"In time, 'twill not. In time, you will beg me to take you, as you begged me before. Aye, *cailin*, you wanted me. You want me now. You cannot deny that—or me."

To show her the truth of his prophetic words, he rolled her over, his dark body sliding inexorably to cover her own pale one, implacably pressing her down and opening her to his desire. A log sparked and broke upon the fire; the candles guttered in their sockets; and beyond the place where the O'Neill and Sionna lay, the storm shuddered and gasped its last, dying breath as he took her again.

This time, he was not gentle. But, lost, once more crying out her surrender, she did not care.

3

SIONNA awoke to a shadowy, midwinter daydream in which she lay in the ancient, decadent bower of some enchanted, fairy-tale tower, where, satiated, effete, she had slept for a hundred years. It was the kiss of her lord and master that stirred her into wakefulness, the touch of his hand upon her breast, the lazy smile of triumph and satisfaction on his lips. All he had charted last night, he now languorously explored anew, his eyes drowsy with sleep and slowly rising passion, while Sionna, only half awake, lay still and breathless and let him do as he wished with her, opening her white thighs wide at the gentle but insistent demand of his hand.

With a long, slow, hard thrust, his seeking manhood found her, pressed deep into her, splitting her and spreading her moist, quicksilver heat. Again and again, he plunged into the liquid warmth of her until her limbs were leaden, her mind was beclouded. In her ear, he whispered with the voice of the wind, as soft as a sigh, stirring her silken tresses. As though it were an ebony skein unwinding, he drew her hair across her throat and then wrapped it about his own, binding them together. He moaned; she gasped, trembling like a butterfly before taking flight to soar across a distant shore where the combers swelled and broke upon obsidian sands, then gently ebbed and died away.

"My lord," Sionna breathed involuntarily, her lashes fluttering open to reveal the startled wonder in her eyes as, at last, he eased himself from her.

"*Mo miann,*" the O'Neill drawled huskily, with a trace of arrogance and amusement. "After last night, did you truly think that 'twas any other?"

In silent, betraying answer, her cheeks stained deeply with crimson at the memory he invoked of his pressing her down and having his will of her, and of her own fervent yielding. Surely, she was a wanton, or mad! she thought. Had she had any pride, any loyalty to her clan at all, she would have waited until he slumbered deep, then crept from his bed, stabbed him with his own dagger, and somehow made good her escape from Ceann-Tíre—not allowed herself to drift into sleep in his warm, secure embrace, replete and exhausted from his lovemaking! What had he done to her that she should have fallen under his devilish spell? She had never felt so bewildered in her life, her mind beset by turmoil, her body by cravings that until last night, she had not even known existed. Now, to her surprise, it seemed strangely that much of her fear of the O'Neill had fled and that it was difficult to summon the intensity of the hatred she had felt toward him before he had claimed her as his.

Sionna's reverie was interrupted by a knock upon the bedchamber door, and at the O'Neill's terse "Come," it swung open to reveal three of the serving maids who had waited upon her the previous evening. They carried buckets of hot water, fresh towels, and her wedding raiment, which had been cleaned and dried. After setting down their burdens and curtsying to the O'Neill, two of the women moved to the windows to draw back the draperies and to open the shutters, which he had finally closed late last night, and to stoke the fire, while the other woman, hands folded, stood in the center of the room to address him.

"My lord, Sir Cullach and the others have returned to Ceann-Tire and do impatiently await your appearance in the great hall to break their fast—for the morn be well advanced—and to learn what you would have them do with the Kilclare woman's beasts and her possessions in the wagon. Besides her horse, there be two great wolfhounds, my lord, which have already attacked and bitten some of the men, and numerous coffers, as well as other things, such as a spinning wheel and a loom."

"First of all," the O'Neill uttered in the low, deceptive voice Sionna was beginning to recognize bespoke barely restrained anger, "you will never again refer to my wife as 'the Kilclare woman.' The Lady

Sionna is an O'Neill and your mistress, and she will be respected and treated as such at all times. Is that clear?" At the woman's startled, frightened nod, he continued coldly. "Very well, then. You may inform Sir Cullach that he's to stable the mare, to chain the dogs in the kennels, and to have the menservants unload the Lady Sionna's belongings and bring them into the great hall, by which time we will be down for the morning meal."

"Aye, my lord."

After curtsying again, all three of the serving maids quickly departed, plainly glad to do so and doubtless eager to be the first downstairs with news of how the O'Neill and his bride had appeared after their wedding night. Sionna was distressed that she should be an object of gossip, but also surprised by and deeply grateful for the O'Neill's unexpected defense of her.

"They—they hate me, you know," she stated quietly. "All of them. I saw it last night, in their eyes. They hoped you would—would hurt me, my lord . . . far more than you—than you did."

"Mayhap," he conceded slowly after a moment. "But you cannot judge them too harshly for that, Sionna. My people have good cause to despise the Kilclares."

He said no more but, after flinging back the bedcovers, rose and strode naked to the washstand, where, after pouring hot water from the pitcher into the basin, he laved his dark visage vigorously, running dripping fingers through his long, unruly black hair to smooth it back from his brow. For a moment, Sionna watched him, marveling at his powerful figure and involuntarily recalling the feel of his hard-muscled body's quickening feverishly against her. Then, realizing where her eyes strayed, she quickly averted her gaze, flushing and mortified yet again by her confused, conflicting emotions toward him, the little tongue of newfound flame that licked through her. To rid herself of her troubling thoughts, she forced herself to examine her surroundings, which looked even more depressing and deteriorated by the light of day. It would be a hard job, putting the keep in order. Still, Sionna was oddly grateful for the task; for she knew that without it, virtually imprisoned here, and having no friends, she would find time hanging heavy on her hands.

"My lord—"

"Lucan. You were not so reticent to call me by name last night, Sionna," the O'Neill reminded her, causing her to blush deeply.

"L-Lucan, then. I—I would know what you— what you expect of me . . . other than what you have already had," she added hastily as, in the polished silver mirror of the washstand, she saw the corners of his mouth lift with mocking amusement. "I would know what my—my place in your household is to be, whether I am to be a—a prisoner here, in this tower, what privileges I am to have . . . if any, what restraints are to be put upon me—" She broke off abruptly, biting her lower lip hard at the thought that she should be compelled to ask these things of her husband.

"Though in a sense you are my captive, my reluctant bride, you are hardly to be a prisoner here. You are my wife, Sionna, and, as such, mistress of Ceann-Tìre. Did I not just say as much to the serving maids? As you can see"—with a sweeping hand, the O'Neill indicated the bedchamber—"there has been no chatelaine here at Ceann-Tìre for many a long year. My mother . . . died when I was but a lad; and my father, like me, having neither the time nor the inclination for household matters, allowed the keep to fall to rack and ruin. Since his death some years ago, most of the repairs to which I've attended have been to the castle's fortifications. I will show you around the fortress later today and give you its keys and ledgers; after that, you may do as you see fit in your domain, my lady—so long as it does not interfere with my own. As for restraints . . . you may not, of course, communicate with the Clan Kilclare; and you may not, without me, go beyond the castle walls. I've a strong suspicion, you see, that you might be tempted to try to run away; and after last night and this morn, I should like that not at all, *mo miann*," he said softly, his amber eyes raking her slowly, significantly.

Then, after kissing her hard and deep, he reluctantly drew away from her and left her. Presently, the serving maids reappeared to help her wash and dress, garbing her in a simple woolen workaday gown that, knowing her wedding costume was far too fine for the chores she planned to undertake, she bade them fetch from one of her coffers that had been borne inside from the wagon. Following that, she joined the O'Neill in his antechamber, where his squires had attended him and from where she and he descended the spiral staircase to the great hall below. There, they broke their fast, Sionna painfully aware of the speculative stares and surreptitious glances of Cullach and the rest of the men as they spied the angry scratches on the O'Neill's cheek and the pale bruise on her own. When, much to her relief, the tense and silent morning meal had ended, she saw to the possessions she had brought with her from Clare Caiseal, instructing the servants to carry her coffers upstairs to the O'Neill's bedchamber, which, he had arrogantly informed her, she was to share with him, and to have none of her own. The spinning wheel and loom she had removed to the solar, which would serve as her private retreat.

Then, as promised, the O'Neill gave her a tour of the castle and presented to her its heavy chatelaine and account books. Only one request did he refuse her: He would not allow Marhalt and Maeve in the donjon, despite that they had enjoyed free run at Clare Caiseal and were not used to being chained in the kennels.

"Wolfhounds are dangerous dogs, my lady," the O'Neill insisted coolly when Sionna dared to protest. "Much more dangerous than you know; and I'll not have them roaming about, attacking my men and the servants."

" 'Twas only because your men are yet unfamiliar to them that Marhalt and Maeve bit them. Please, my lord, my dogs are not accustomed to being penned—"

"Do not press me on this, Sionna, I warn you," he rejoined darkly, his face growing impassive as he stared at her from beneath hooded lids. "You are more fortunate than you know that I permit you to keep them at all!"

Understanding then that she dared not press him, Sionna accepted his decision without further demurring. Already, he had granted to her far more than she had ever hoped; to ask for still more was to risk having it all taken away. Having completed showing her the majority of the fortress, the O'Neill then went about his business, as she did hers, calling the servants together and explaining what she wanted of them in the future as far as the household was concerned. Though they yet eyed her slyly and hostilely, it was clear that word of the O'Neill's proclaiming her mistress of Ceann-Tìre had rapidly spread; presently, stout menservants armed with rush rakes were hard at work removing the filthy straw that covered the floor of the great hall, and the serving maids were equally occupied with their scrub brushes and pails of sudsy water, no man or woman refusing to heed Sionna's dictates. It was not to be expected, of course, that the keep could be put to rights in a single afternoon. But a start was made that was to set the pattern of Sionna's coming days—just as her wedding night was to set the pattern for all the nights that followed.

For where she was concerned, the O'Neill was insatiable, his desire for her bordering on obsession. No matter how many times he took her, he would never have enough of her, he knew instinctively, so rare was her beauty, so alluring was her body. There was nothing he did not know, did not teach her as the slow winter nights passed. He initiated her well and thoroughly in the rites of lovemaking. Time and time again, he pressed her down upon his canopy bed in the tower to work his dark, enthralling magic upon her, until she knew every plane and angle of his hard, powerful body as well as she knew the soft, seductive curves of her own. There were languid, protracted nights when he teased and tormented her at his leisure, erotically, almost cruelly, until, despite herself, she begged him to take her; and barbarous, unbridled nights when, long after she had fallen asleep, he roused her to force himself on her urgently, savagely, without any preliminaries. Inevitably in the end, no matter how much she might have wished otherwise, she was lost, helpless against him, his to do with as he pleased, swept away by whatever dark, wild, earthy thing he loosed inside her, shocking and shaming her, burning and exalting her.

Yet, to her surprise, Sionna discovered as the days passed that she was not discontent. Though she had not expected it, she and the O'Neill had much in common, both emotionally and intellectually, a shared passion for bard song and poetry, a mutual interest in politics and, closer to home, farming and related household affairs. He devoted much of his time to his land and tenants, while Sionna proved herself a competent chatelaine, bringing order and cleanliness to the castle as she worked to restore it. Often in the evenings, he played the harp and sang for her as she embroidered by the light of the fire, or they played cards or chess together, each finding much to like and to admire in the other. He talked to her in a manner Ruaidhri never had, as though she were his equal, and he frequently consulted her about this matter or that, respecting the opinions she voiced. In fact, the O'Neill behaved so consistently as though theirs was a love match that Sionna found herself forgetting he was her enemy and growing closer to him than she had ever been to any man. It was as though she had known him forever, had always shared his bed; and sometimes, startling her, she could hardly remember her life before he had come into it, could not imagine it without him.

And so Sionna's days and nights passed, one much like another until the day when, just before sundown, the O'Neill abruptly vanished without a word from Ceann-Tìre, leaving Sionna alone among his kinsmen and servants. She was startled to descend to the great hall for supper and to find him absent; she was stricken to be informed by Cullach that the lord and master of Ceann-Tìre would not be joining them for the evening meal. For the O'Neill alone stood between her and those at the castle, and a frisson of fear crept up her spine at the thought of facing them without him at her side. Panicking her utterly was the sudden, terrible suspicion that the O'Neill, having taken what he wanted from her, now had deliberately forsaken her, callously delivering her unto the hands of his men for sport, as he had once coldly threatened to do. Horrified, Sionna would have run to their bedchamber and locked and barred the door tight, then stood with his mighty *claidheamh mór* in hand to defend her honor and life. But Cullach was already pulling out the thronelike chair for her at the head table and bidding her to sit down. Shuddering, she sat.

"You've no need to be afraid, my lady," he said as he seated himself beside her, in his customary place, leaving the O'Neill's great chair empty. "All here know how you've bewitched the O'Neill, how he is so besotted with you that he would slay any man who was mad or fool enough to dare to lay a hand on you. So be at ease. No man here will harm you."

But Sionna found Cullach's words cold comfort, especially when it gradually dawned on her that she was the only female present in the great hall. The wives of the O'Neill's few married kinsmen were nowhere to be seen; nor did any serving maids wait upon the tables. Only the menservants stood close at hand.

"Cullach, where—where are all the women?" she asked anxiously, alarmed.

"At their own hearths or other duties, my lady," he responded evenly enough; but still, she sensed he lied, and her dread increased.

During her father's absences from the great hall of Clare Caiseal, the atmosphere had always been more relaxed, the men more boisterous, the women gayer. Strangely, this was not the case at Ceann-Tìre. Instead of appearing relieved by the absence of the lord and master whom they seemed to behold with such fear, the O'Neill's men were even more surly and taciturn than usual, the atmosphere of the great hall tense, uneasy, silent save for the men's occasional low mutterings, the clink of dinner daggers upon platters, and the scrape of benches upon the stone floor strewn with fresh rushes. Even the animals were restive; for in the distance, borne on the wind, Sionna could hear from the stables the nervous whickering and stamping of the horses and, from the kennels, the ferocious barking of Marhalt and Maeve amid that of the O'Neill's smaller hunting dogs. The seabirds along the shore shrieked, their high-pitched calls fearful and forlorn; and a lone hawk screamed in the night. Startlingly near, it seemed, a wolf bayed at the moon, a strangely horrific, haunting howl that sent an icy grue up Sionna's spine; and from far away rose an eerie, answering wail.

The hurriedly eaten supper ended, and the men quickly departed from the great hall, all save Cullach, who stayed behind to escort Sionna to her room.

"Sleep well, my lady," he murmured, a curious light in his eyes as they paused before her doorway. It seemed for a moment as though he would speak further; but, instead, he silently bowed low and kissed her hand, then turned on his booted heel and left her.

Much to her relief, when she entered the bedchamber, Sionna saw that the three serving maids she had chosen permanently to wait upon her were there, with a bath already prepared for her and her night rail and wrapper laid out upon the bed. As they did each night, the women bathed and powdered and perfumed her, then clothed her in the wispy nightgown and robe. But though they had gradually grown more garrulous in her presence, tonight, oddly, they spoke little and rushed her through her toilette, as though eager to be gone. More than once, as the wild barking and baying and howling outside continued, they exchanged grim, apprehensive glances; and after they had departed, she chanced to overhear them conversing beyond her doorway, the wind carrying the sound of their low, cryptic words to her ears.

"She may have cast her witch's spell upon the O'Neill, aye; but let us see now if she be powerful enough and so willing and eager to charm the other—"

"*If* he comes—"

"He *will* come . . . sooner or later; for has he not managed it before? Aye, he grows ever stronger and more cunning, methinks, and the O'Neill less able to curb him . . ."

"If that be true—"

"Aye, 'twill bode ill for us all, for 'twill be as 'twas in the old days, when the old *tòiseach* was alive, when there was rape and mayhem and murder committed beyond these stone walls—and within, the blood never to be washed clean . . . 'Tis well she be here, I say. Let *her* have a taste of what we have lived with all these long, terrible years; let *her* suffer as we have suffered the curse of the Kilclare witch, Igrania—may her black soul be damned and rot in hell for all eternity!"

"We have done what we could. Let us hope and pray 'tis enough."

"Well, I for one pity her—"

"Faith! Art a fool, then! I say: Better *her* than one of us, one of our own . . ."

At that, the serving maids moved away, and Sionna's ears perceived no more, much to her anguish and chagrin. Although she had not fully comprehended the dialogue, what she had heard had chilled her to the very marrow of her bones. It had seemed to indicate that some unknown malevolence was directed toward her, that some unknown "other," whom even the O'Neill had difficulty restraining, wished her injury. Shivering uncontrollably in her thin nightgown and robe, she moved slowly to stand before the fire in the hearth, wishing fervently, for the first time in the weeks since her arrival at Ceann-Tìre, that the O'Neill would come, would enfold her in his strong, protective arms and lay her down upon the bed, his body like a shield covering her own. If Cullach had spoken truly, then the O'Neill would let no harm come to her from any man. But the O'Neill had disappeared, and she was alone at Ceann-Tìre, with some unknown someone who apparently wished her ill . . .

Jolted from her reverie by the sudden slam of an outer door, followed by a spate of cursing in the inner ward, Sionna ran to the window and, looking out, observed Cullach striding across the bailey, carrying some burden she could not distinguish in the darkness. As the O'Neill's *tànaiste*, Cullach had apartments in the donjon rather than in the barracks over the stables. Yet despite the late hour, he, too, was abandoning the now eerily deserted keep, leaving her alone . . . Terrified by the realization, Sionna grabbed up her sable mantle and, flinging it about her shoulders, raced from the bedchamber, down the spiral staircase, and through the great hall, out into the night.

"Cullach! Cullach, wait!" she cried.

"What do you here, my lady?" he asked sharply, suspiciously, upon turning to see her running toward him, her long, unbound hair streaming wildly from her face, her cape half parted to reveal her white night rail and robe, their diaphanous folds seeming to flutter wraithlike about her. "God's blood!" he hissed, stricken and glancing uneasily about. "You are barefoot and half naked under your cloak! Do you not know what the O'Neill would do to us both if he spied us here together, and you in such a state of undress? He would rend us limb from limb, slay us where we stand! Go back inside at once!"

"Nay! I am afraid! Something is wrong! The servants have fled, and I am all alone—Cullach! What is happening? Where is Lucan? Where are you going? You are the *tànaiste* of Ceann-Tìre. 'Tis your bounden duty to guard me, the wife of your *tòiseach*, in his absence!"

"I do not need you to remind me of my duty, my lady! 'Tis but to quiet the damned dogs I go." He indicated the load he bore, which she now saw was a platter piled high with raw mutton haunches from several recently slaughtered sheep. "Their bloody racket is enough to wake the devil—and your own two wolfhounds the worst of the lot, inciting all the rest, I swear. Why the O'Neill ever permitted you to bring them here, I'm sure I'm not knowing! 'Twas a mad thing, in truth! Now, do you go back inside, ere you take a chill—or tempt me into forgetting 'tis the O'Neill's wife you are—witch, sorceress!" His gray eyes narrowed as they swept over her appraisingly, glinting like the silver blade of his claymore in the diffuse light cast by the pale-glowing moon in the night sky.

She could not trust Cullach, Sionna thought then, not only because of the way he looked at her, but also because when his windblown cloak swirled back from his shoulders, she saw that he was not only armed, but also armored—to feed the dogs! Surely, even her wolfhounds were not so savage as that!

Hysterical laughter bubbled in her throat. With difficulty, she choked it down; and as reason slowly prevailed, she recognized that Cullach must intend to ride beyond the castle walls. Whom did he go to meet? The "other"? Or mayhap he *was* the other, bent on seizing her and Ceann-Tìre both for himself! It would not be the first time such a power struggle had taken place within a clan. If such a battle were indeed in the offing, the servants would know, as they always knew everything; perhaps they were even now barricaded in their own quarters downstairs in the basement, hoping to escape bloodshed.

Gasping, Sionna whirled and fled, her breath coming in hard rasps as she sped back inside the donjon and up to her bedchamber, slamming the door shut behind her and leaning against it weakly, shaking with cold and fear as she sought to catch her breath. There was no one to help her, she realized with a sinking heart, no one to defend her against whatever assault might be attempted upon her this night. For she felt certain such was intended. In the O'Neill's absence, his men and servants betrayed her! As the idea occurred to her, Sionna was violently tempted to lock and to bar her door. She was deterred only by the thought of the O'Neill's wrath should he return home to find himself prevented from entering his own room. For that, he would doubtless beat her; and surely, she must be wrong about her dreadful suspicions. Surely, no matter how much the servants hated her, no man at Ceann-Tíre would dare to lift a hand against the wife of their lord and master! Yet she remembered the look in Cullach's own eyes when he had assessed her, and she trembled. Throwing off her mantle, she paced the floor agitatedly, greatly relieved when all the ruckus being raised by the dogs at last quieted.

Surprisingly famished, Sionna strode to the side table and helped herself to some bread and meat and cheese from the cold repast that had been laid out. Quickly and nervously, she crammed the food into her mouth, scarcely even noticing that the roast beef was undercooked again, though she had chided the cook several times for such. Her ears remained sharply attuned to every creak and groan of the ancient fortress, her dinner dagger comfortably close at hand. But as her belly grew replete, and, still, nothing untoward happened, Sionna began to calm herself, to feel foolishly that perhaps she had indeed let her fear and imagination run away with her. The wine she had drunk with her small meal was proving unusually soporific, as well, making it hard for her to stay alert and dulling her fright considerably.

Finally, not knowing what else to do, she climbed into bed and, shoving her dinner dagger under her pillow for protection, pulled the covers about her. Her eyelids drooped shut, and she drifted toward slumber. But as she half slept, half dreamed, she found herself beset by a different sort of restlessness. She was dimly aware that the dogs had started barking and baying once more; the wolves she had heard earlier howled in reply, the fierce, feral sound uncanny and unnerving, yet somehow oddly painful and lonesome, as well; and as she lay in the bed she and the O'Neill had shared together every night since their wedding, she longed for him. She ached to feel his mouth and tongue and hands upon her, stirring and sating her. Her body, flushed and hot and wakened so completely to desire and delight, now craved him like a drug. Fitfully, she tossed and turned, murmuring his name, "Lucan . . . Lucan . . . " and instinctively seeking easement for what ailed her. But there was none to be found.

The O'Neill did not come.

Despite herself, Sionna was deeply wounded by the unbidden thought that perhaps he had tired of her already and lay even now in the arms of another woman. A solitary tear slipped down her cheek as she slept and dreamed that her heart was made of crystal—and was shattering into small and painful shards inside her.

4

"**D**ON'T touch me, you . . . you brute, you beast!" Sionna hissed angrily, as she suddenly came wide awake and realized the O'Neill lay naked beside her in the bed and was kissing and caressing her lightly, so as to quicken her desire before she had yet fully roused.

So he often did, causing her to awaken on the verge of climax, to the feel of him entering her smoothly, sliding deep inside her the moment she opened her midnight-blue eyes, making her gasp and moan and cry out as he crushed her to him fiercely, groaning and shuddering against her, his own peak coming as swiftly as hers. Afterward, maddening and shaming her, he would smile down at her mockingly, his golden eyes gleaming at the shared knowledge of how quickly and easily he bestirred her body when her mind offered no resistance.

But this morning, Sionna had awakened too soon, and now, determined that he should not take her that way, that he should not take her at all after last night, she fought him. Clenched fists flying up without warning, she pummeled his massive chest and attempted to push him off her. When the O'Neill swore, surprised, and instinctively grabbed her wrists tight, she began twisting and writhing beneath him, seeking to escape and crying out, "Let

me go! Let me go, damn you! Bastard!''—to no avail.
With one hand, he calmly, cavalierly, pinned her
arms behind her back and, with the other, forced
her stubbornly defiant chin up so he could see her
flushed, scowling face, her sapphire-blue eyes that
stabbed daggers at him.

"May I know the reason for this sudden, un-
seemly, and, of course, quite futile—attempt to deny
me my rights as your husband, my lady?'' the
O'Neill inquired coolly. His hand strayed deliberately, insolently, over her ripe, heaving breasts, then
lower still, to tug gently at soft, silken black curls
and to trail idly along the insides of her thighs. His
amber eyes glittered speculatively and—curiously,
Sionna thought—even a trifle warily as he stared
down at her, his body oddly taut and still as he
awaited her reply, only his hand moving, continuing
to stroke her.

"Oh!" she gasped, outraged, trembling with fury
and unwilling arousal. "Do not try to play me for a
fool, my lord, that you need must ask me that! How
dare you leave me all alone here last night—knowing how your men and the servants loathe me and
never saying a word to me as to your whereabouts
or when to expect your return! How dare you come
to my bed straight from that of your mistress, your
whore! You are a cocksure fool, in truth, if 'twas
willing you thought to find me!"

"Why, Sionna, *mo miann*, I do believe that you actually missed me," the O'Neill uttered softly, the
tenseness in his body dissolving and his eyes now
filled with a peculiar, eager, searching light that puzzled her, his mouth curving in an enigmatic smile
that, while startling—for she had fully expected him
to be enraged by her vehement tirade and resistance—nevertheless made Sionna long to do him
some injury. "I do believe that you're jealous!"

She was shocked by the notion.

"Nay! I'm not! Of—of course, I'm not!" she insisted, though she found that she could no longer meet his penetrating gaze and that, to her embarrassment, her cheeks stained betrayingly with color. "Why—why should I be? I'd sooner you bedded down with any woman but me!"

"Now that, *mo miann*, is a lie," he drawled thickly as he slowly lowered his head once more to kiss her. "As I certainly intend to prove ... "

He made love to her twice. In between, when Sionna finally admitted to him how frightened she had been last night, he smoothly allayed her fears, informing her that the wives of his few married men occasionally preferred to sup in their own apartments, that it had long been the custom of his servants to retire early during his absence from the keep, and that she was surely mistaken about the serving maids' conversation she had overheard.

"There is no man here at Ceann-Tíre but I who shall ever touch you, Sionna, I swear!" He spoke quietly but savagely, his eyes shuttered so she could not guess his thoughts—though, for a moment, his hands tightened on her so painfully that she knew they would leave bruises, and she could have sworn there was a look of utter anguish and torment upon his dark visage. "Cullach is right," he continued. "You've no need to fear my men or the servants." Moments later, however, whatever she had glimpsed upon his face was gone as quickly as it had seemed to appear, leading her to believe that perhaps it had been nothing more than a trick of the shadowy, wintry morning light, after all; and she forgot all about it when his mouth closed hungrily again over hers.

There was one thing, however, that the O'Neill did not explain to her—his absence from the keep.

Nor, to Sionna's deep, inexplicable hurt, did he deny having been with a mistress, a whore. So the second time, some four weeks later, when he again disappeared without a word, she felt certain it was to seek out arms other than her own; and when he vanished from the keep yet a third time in as many months, she was sure her rival was a mistress of long standing, whom he visited on a regular basis. Sionna taxed him no further about the matter, however, realizing that had he intended to give her an explanation for his forays, he would have done so from the start; and she did not want him to think she was jealous, as he had charged. Jealousy implied caring—and she did not care about him, her husband, her enemy; she did not!

As was their apparent custom, the servants continued to retire early on the occasions of their lord and master's absence, leaving her all alone. But now, tonight, because nothing untoward had ever occurred, Sionna felt hardly any fear, only a peculiar loneliness as she sat in one of the window seats of her tower room, gazing out over the eastern sea and listening to the sounds of the darkness. The shrill, aching call of the seabirds that sailed on the night wind. The lapping of the dark, frothy waves against the shore of the promontory from which Ceann-Tìre rose, and against the causeway that joined it to the mainland. The thud of the great-hall doors when Cullach left the donjon to feed the restive dogs; the abrupt fading of their baying into stillness before, after a time, they began again, doubtless quarreling over the bones. The whisper of the wind as it swept across the sea and moors and crept through the passage of the keep. The skittering of the mice as they darted from their hiding places to snatch crumbs that had fallen from the trestle tables in the great hall. The snap and crackle of the logs that broke upon the blaze in the hearth; the soft hiss of the flames when the wind sighed down the massive flue, causing pale tendrils of smoke to wreathe the bed-chamber. The haunting, forlorn howls of the wolves that stalked the long-shadowed forests and hunted across the moors hazy with mist, and the terrible, tortured cry of one wolf who was nearer than the rest, the one Sionna had come to think of as the strangest and saddest of them all.

Shivering at the sound, she slowly rose and, after extinguishing the candles one by one, climbed into bed, dizzy and drowsy from the wine she had drunk, which always seemed curiously more potent and enervating during the O'Neill's absences. Yet for all that, she could not get comfortable, but tossed and turned restlessly for hours, it seemed, feeling fitful and flushed, as though she were beset by a fever. Her body burned with a fire that yearned to be quenched, as it always did when the O'Neill did not return home until morning; and at last, scarcely even aware she did so, Sionna impatiently tore off her night rail and cast it aside, finding the sheets' welcome coolness soothing against her nakedness. Finally, she drifted into slumber and dreamed a deeply disturbing dream—a dark, erotic nightmare.

She dreamed that sometime in the night, the door to her bedchamber swung slowly open on creaking hinges to reveal someone, some*thing*, standing upon the threshold, watching her and panting as though he had run a very long way. After a moment, the nails of his padded feet clicking softly upon the oaken floor, the thing prowled into the tower and came to a halt beside her bed. When, as though she somehow sensed his presence, she was wakened and her eyelids fluttered open, Sionna saw by the dim, wavering light of the low-burning fire that it was neither man nor beast who loomed above her, but

somehow both. It was as though the eerie, elongated
shadows that blurred and darkened the edges of the
circular room played tricks upon her eyes.

The creature's sleek head bore the upper face of
an immense wolf, the largest she had ever seen,
black fur fading into a handsome silver mask about
his glowing, predatory eyes and partial muzzle that
blended so smoothly with the lower half of a man's
dark and heavily stubbled visage that the two im-
ages seemed somehow as one. His front legs were
those of a wolf, as well, with enormous paws as big
as a man's hands and tipped with sharp black claws.
But the beast stood upright, with the tall, powerful
body and hard, heavy sex of a man. Naked and rippling with muscle, he was so dark and hirsute that
it seemed his massive chest matted with velvety
black hair flowed into the glossy black pelt of his
arms and shoulders and face, making it difficult to
distinguish where man ended and beast began—or
perhaps both were one and the same, Sionna
thought dumbly as she gazed up at him, morbidly
fascinated despite her fear. Though his bushy, silver-
tipped black tail that brushed the floor was plainly
discernible, his hind legs appeared to be those of a
man one moment, those of a wolf the next, indeter-
minate, like the rest of him, confusing her, making
her doubt what her startled eyes beheld. Like something to be found only in a nightmare, dredged only
from the darkest chasms of her subconscious, the
man-beast was—huge, frightening, dangerous, magnificent, exuding lethal animal menace and
magnetism, treacherously carnal and seductive, a
throwback to some atavistic time, some primal place
of magic and mystery and mystic standing stones.
So the pagan druids of the ancient Celtic tribes must
have looked, Sionna realized in some cranny of her
beclouded brain, when, cloaked in their animal

skins, they had become as mythic shapeshifters, sub-
tly taking on the appearance and characteristics of
the beasts they had portrayed, seeming to metamor-
phose into the actual creatures themselves.

For a long, horrifying moment in her dream, the
man-beast did naught but stare down at her silently,
rapaciously, his gleaming eyes hypnotizing her, par-
alyzing her, as those of a predator rivet its prey a
heartbeat before the kill. Then, without warning,
snarling low in his throat, he suddenly sprang upon
her, releasing her from his demonic, binding spell.
Utterly terrified then, driven by pure survival in-
stinct, Sionna screamed and screamed again as he
fell upon her, his harsh breath hot against her throat,
his mighty arms and legs hemming her in on both
sides as he crouched over her cringing figure. In her
dream, no one at Ceann-Tìre heard her cries, or if
they did, they ignored them—or perhaps she only
thought she screamed and, in reality, made no
sound at all, as is the way of a nightmare.

Desperately, she tried at first to flee and then to
fight the wolfish creature, to defend herself against
him. But to her consternation, Sionna discovered she
was peculiarly dazed and lethargic, as though she
were ill or drunk or drugged. She seemed to move
in slow motion, as though her mind and will no
longer had any control over her body. She could not
escape. Her pitiful attempt to contest the man-beast
was futile, easily overcome when he captured her
wrists in a bruising clench and dragged them beneath her, pinioning them tight with one padded
paw. As he did so, he compelled her back to arch
enticingly, her breasts to strain upward, her nipples
to tremble with unwitting allurement against his
broad, furry chest, her hips to thrust temptingly
against his own, her silky womanhood to brush his
potent sex. She shivered with both terror and an in-

voluntary, leaping, melting response that shocked and shamed her utterly. She felt she was but a heartbeat from death—or worse. Her blood pounded so fiercely that it was as though it would burst from her veins. Whimpering, she thrashed her dizzied head, instinctively baring her swanlike throat, exposing its pale, vulnerable length to the wolfish creature, in an age-old gesture of appeasement and submission. She expected he would rip out her jugular vein at any moment.

But when he finally lowered his dusky, handsome head to her throat, it was to lick her there, a long, languorous lick that followed the graceful arch of her throat from its base upward and that, despite her dread, sent a wild, depraved anticipation shuddering through her entire body. At that, the man-beast drew back a little so he could see her face, his glimmering eyes boring down into hers, smoldering with a dark and dangerous hunger that made her breath catch on a ragged sob as she understood his desire and intent.

Once more, she struggled dully to marshal her wits, to wrest free from him, to battle him—in vain. He subjugated her utterly. Giddy and weak, she was powerless against his great strength as he pressed her down, still holding her prisoner with one paw, while the other began to roam over her, discovering and caressing her and bestirring her young, vital body, which had been so thoroughly and expertly wakened by the O'Neill and was eager and unsated in his absence. She felt the wolfish creature's torrid breath against her ear and upon her sultry skin as he nuzzled and sniffed her, teasing her earlobe, trailing slowly across her cheek and down her neck to her breasts, where he inhaled deeply the sweet, wild, musky fragrance of her. The feral, forest scent seemed to inflame him. His mouth found the sensitive place on her shoulder where it joined her nape, and he bit her there gently. His rough tongue stabbed her with its heat, causing another tremulous thrill to shoot through her and making her cry out obliviously against him, a low, animalistic moan that Sionna was only dimly aware came from her own throat.

She could not believe that this was happening to her, that this was real. Then she remembered that it was not, that it was only a dream, a nightmare, however fantastic and fearsome and fervent. Still, no matter how hard she tried, she could not seem to awaken from it, to drive the man-beast from her mind. She had never before had such a graphic, concupiscent dream, in which all her senses seemed to play such a large part. She could see the wolfish creature bending over her, his sleek, powerful muscles rippling and quivering sinuously as he twined himself about her, as the smoke from the fire curled like gossamer mist about the bedchamber, giving it a surrealistic quality, until the intricately carved posts of the enormous bed seemed to resemble the trunks of ancient, gnarled trees and its canopy their spreading boughs. She could hear his soft growls and pants as he explored her, growing ever more excited as, of its own accord, her vibrant body roused and responded to his increasingly bolder advances, bucking and writhing beneath him. She could smell the scent of him, like that of her own fragrance, only stronger, muskier, woodsier, so the two mingled together and permeated the tower; and it seemed in her dream that where she and the man-beast lay was the wild, shadowed forest, upon sweet, soft grasses crushed and trampled to release their green perfume. She could taste him when, ensnaring his paw in her tangled hair, he raised her head to press it against his sweat-dampened chest,

his fleecy flesh salty upon her lips. She could feel his
unstill mouth and tongue, his teeth and free paw
everywhere upon her, licking and pillaging, nipping
and petting, heightening her passion and deepening
her chagrin that she should be so highly and provocatively stimulated by him. Sionna prayed the
wolfish creature would soon be done with her, but
to her despair, he was not so inclined.

He stroked her breasts until they ached passion,
and her sensitive nipples grew taut and hard beneath his relentless, taunting tongue. He drew his
claws lightly, like rough, raw silk, down her qua-
vering belly and along the insides of her trembling
thighs, sending tingles surging through her whole
body. Endlessly, it seemed, he tormented her, scat-
tering her senses, leaving her faint and breathless,
floating in a dark, timeless place and filled with fear
and a perverse, perilous excitement that horrified
and humiliated her, even as it ignited a wildly burning fire of desire in her blood.

Time passed. Sionna did not know how much
time, though in her dream it seemed an eternity in
which she drifted and throbbed and lusted for the
man-beast to take her, to satisfy what he had
wrought within her—so skillfully and savagely that
she felt she was become an animal herself, a she-wolf
in season and frantic to be mated. They were bathed
with sweat. Their bodies glistened in the red-gold
glow of the firelight that dimly illuminated the shadowy bedchamber, she pale, he dark as he slid ag-
gressively across her, panting in her ear, growling
low against her throat, his turgid sex a portentous
threat, a beguiling promise as his devouring mouth
and lapping tongue swept lower still, scalding her
belly and thighs before, at long last, he ruthlessly
opened her. Brazenly, the wolfish creature tasted
her, his tongue dipping deep into the dark, secret

heart of her, then cleaving her swollen nether lips to spread sweet-flowing honey lingeringly along their soft, trembling folds as he teased into unfurling the tightly closed bud that was the key to her delight. Again and again, he repeated the quickening, feverish motion until, despite herself, Sionna whimpered and strained like a mad thing beneath him, desperate for release.

At that, the paw that fastened her hands behind her back tugged upon them insistently, compelling her slowly to turn over, while the other paw slipped beneath her belly to lift her hips so her face was pressed against the pillow. Then, poised behind her, the man-beast swiftly spread her yielding thighs wide and urgently mounted her, his sex thrusting suddenly and powerfully and fully into her, the force of his barbarous entry making her gasp and cry out, low, hoarse wails of surrender as she felt the welcome hardness, the rapturous heaviness plunge slickly between her thighs, filling her to overflowing. She was consumed by passion, spurred by desire as, supporting himself on one paw, the other wrapped tightly around her waist, the wolfish creature drove hard and deep into her, again and again, his breath coming in heated rasps against her nape, his chest pressed against her back as he rocked her faster and faster, until she was gasping for air and shuddering uncontrollably from the violent, frenzied climax that rapidly erupted inside her. His own release came as quickly and explosively as hers, and with a fierce, exultant howl, he spilled himself inside her, crushing her against him brutally until he was finally spent.

For a moment, they knelt there locked together still, panting, hearts pounding. Then, at last, the man-beast withdrew from her and, giving a low, purring growl of triumph and satisfaction, lay down beside her, curling himself around her protectively

and briefly nuzzling and licking her ear to show her
how much she had pleased him. Replete and exhausted, Sionna slept deeply in his possessive embrace—and dreamed of being wakened later to be
savagely taken by him again and yet again before,
finally sated, he padded silently from her bedchamber just before dawn.

5

WHEN Sionna awoke late the following morning, it was to find that for the first time since
their marriage, the O'Neill did not lie beside her in
their bed and that the tower was so cold that she
shivered beneath the bedcovers. She thought dimly
that the fire in the hearth must have gone out—or
perhaps she had simply grown accustomed to the
O'Neill's big, powerful body wrapped around her,
warming her. Still, despite his absence, she had not
been cold last night, she thought, confused, a dark
and disturbing memory stirring deep in her. Then,
in a torrid rush, her bizarre, erotic dream of last
night flooded her mind, causing her to gasp with
shock and shame. Surely, she must be a wanton,
Sionna thought, horrified—nay, worse! She must be
mad and depraved!

Stricken, she sat up slowly in the bed, instinctively
clutching the bedcovers to her body as she discovered she was utterly naked, as she knew she would
have been had she awakened in the O'Neill's em-

brace. But he was not beside her; and for a moment, bewildered and terrified, she thought that perhaps her dream had been no nightmare, after all, but had happened in truth. Then, as she glanced feverishly about the chilly room, she saw to her vast relief that the O'Neill had opened the northern doors of the tower and stood, naked and legs spread wide, upon the balcony, his head flung back, his long, shaggy black hair streaming from his dark visage in the wind, his arms uplifted and outstretched as though in supplication. On his unguarded face was such an expression of suffering and torment that Sionna was frightened.

"My lord!" she exclaimed, alarmed, springing from the bed, haphazardly dragging a sheet about her to cover her nakedness against the frigid air as she ran to him. "My lord! Lucan . . . Lucan, what is it? What's wrong?" The words tumbled from her lips as, impulsively enfolding her arms about him, she pressed herself against his back, laying her head upon his shoulder. "Are you ill?"

"Aye," he muttered fiercely, brokenly, a long, violent shudder racking his hard-muscled body. "I am ill unto death! Oh, Sionna! Sionna!" he suddenly cried out, an anguished wail, as he turned and clasped her to him tightly, his fingers snarling in her hair, compelling her to bury her face against his chest.

For a long moment, the O'Neill held her thus, while her heart beat hard and fast in her breast, with dread that there should be aught wrong with him, with the sudden, agonizing realization of what her life would be without him—brutal and bleak and utterly bereft. So deeply painful, in fact, was the thought of never again feeling his arms about her so, never again feeling his powerful body pressing her down, that Sionna knew deep in her heart that no matter how hard she had tried to fight against it, she had fallen irrevocably in love with him, her enemy, her husband.

"Lucan, what is it? What is wrong?" she queried again, glad he could not see the sudden tears that glistened in her eyes at the bittersweet knowledge that her love should be forever unrequited. For to him, she knew, she would never be other than a Kilclare witch, his captive bride, claimed and conquered and kept by him like a trophy. "What illness has beset you, my lord?"

" 'Tis naught. 'Tis naught!" he repeated fiercely, as though to convince himself as well as her, his face so grim that it scared her. "No more than a black mood that does come upon me now and then. I do but brood, that is all. Do not trouble yourself about it, my lady."

"But I—but I *do* trouble myself, my lord." Sionna's voice trembled with fear and love and hurt that he had spoken so harshly. "You are my—my husband. If aught is wrong, I should know of it."

"Aye, perhaps. But there is naught you can do for me, my lady—or so you said once. I am accursed, and I must live with that, it seems. I had hoped otherwise, not only for my own sake, but also for yours, Sionna. For sometimes, the curse weighs so heavily upon me that I . . . that I am . . . not myself—" He broke off abruptly, a muscle flexing in his taut jaw. Then, after a moment, his voice low and impassioned, he said, "I do not want to hurt you, *mo miann*, and sometimes, I fear I shall, for we O'Neills of Clandeboye are a brutal lot, and I've the devil's own temper . . . Nay, let it be, Sionna," he muttered roughly when she would have spoken again. " 'Tis but a black mood, as I have told you, and it fills my mind with strange fancies . . . 'Twill pass. 'Twill pass . . .

"Come, you are shaking from the cold," he continued. "Though spring comes quickly, I should not have opened the balcony doors. But sometimes, I need must feel the elements—the wild wind, the mist, the spindrift—upon my face and against my bare skin. They do help to clear my mind of the dark thoughts that plague me . . . Come," he insisted again. "Let me take you inside to the fire, where you may warm yourself."

So saying, the O'Neill caught Sionna up in his arms and carried her into the tower, where he laid her down upon the bed. Then, after tossing more wood onto the fire, which had burned low during the night, he slipped in beside her. But to her surprise, though he drew her close against him, he did not make love to her, seeming content simply to hold her silently until, warmed by the heat of his body, she drifted once more into slumber. When she again awoke, he was gone; and that night when he came to her—and for many long nights afterward— the O'Neill was so strangely gentle when he took her that Sionna knew what it was to be kissed by the clouds and to feel the winds of heaven soft upon her skin.

But at last, there arrived once more a night when he absented himself from the keep; and she slept and dreamed fitfully, feverishly, as she had before, and in her dream, the man-beast padded stealthily into her bedchamber to claim her hard and savagely again, making her gasp and shudder and cry out hoarsely, like an animal. The next morning, when she awoke and, rising, chanced to glimpse her reflection in her polished silver mirror, Sionna saw that she was wan and worn—her midnight-blue eyes were ringed with mauve circles, like bruises— as though she had hardly slept at all; and she was disturbed and frightened to recall that this time, the powerful, erotic nightmare had seemed somehow even stronger, more real than before.

So vivid was this impression, in fact, that she was half tempted to tell the O'Neill of the dusky, wolfish creature who had begun to haunt her strange, smoke-filled dreams of fiery passion. But in the end, she did not—not only because, loving him, she did not want him to think she was mad and perverted, but also because over the past two months, he had seemed to grow increasingly withdrawn and brooding, his mood so curiously dark and afflicted that his men and the servants crept about the fortress even more fearfully than before, starting at sounds and shadows, as though monsters lurked in every corner.

Sionna herself was as tense and disquieted as the rest; for it had seemed to her ever since she had arrived at Ceann-Tìre that some peculiar pall lay upon the castle—the curse, if legend spoke truly, of her ancestor, the witch, Igrania of Clare Caiseal. Now, Sionna thought uneasily that whatever dreadful, baleful, unknown thing gripped the keep, it was slowly but surely tightening its malignant hold.

A month later, yet a third time in the O'Neill's absence did the man-beast come to her while she slept and dreamed her explicit, carnal nightmare; and this time, when he lay with her, such was his ferocity that he raked his claws across her tender flesh and then, slowly lowering his head to the gouges, licked away the blood that stained her snow-white breast. And this time, when she awakened in the morning, Sionna knew at long last that it was no dream, but a dark and terrible reality. For when she chanced again upon rising to glimpse her reflection in her polished silver mirror, she saw to her utter horror that five deep scratches marred her pale skin.

She was shocked and sickened and shamed by the hideous realization that hands other than the O'Neill's had touched her, had defiled and degraded her, and, worse, that she had reveled in it like an animal. She was violently ill in the chamber pot, too distressed even to notice that, for the first morning since their marriage, the O'Neill was not present in the tower. Afterward, it was a long time before she slowly staggered upright. Trembling as though with fever, she struggled into her wrapper and, her shaking hands clutching its folds tight about her, made her way to sit on a low stool before the fire, unable to bear even the thought of lying down once more in the bed where she had been savagely taken again and again by the man-beast. For a long while, she huddled there upon the stone hearth, shivering and whimpering, dwelling numbly on the violation that had been done to her; and it was thus that the O'Neill found her.

"Sionna!" he cried upon entering the tower. "Sionna!"

Terrified, she tried to turn away, to cover herself as he strode toward her, then gathered her in his arms. But it was too late; she heard him inhale sharply and saw the look in his eyes when he observed the gouges upon her. He would kill her, she thought, believing her unfaithful to him! Cowering, she waited for him to do her some mortal violence; and when he did not, when he instead slowly lowered his head and gently kissed the wounds, she understood at last the essence of the terrible curse that afflicted him.

"'Twas *you*, Lucan!" she breathed. "'Twas you who put these marks upon me! *You* are the man-beast!" Though she was shocked and horrified to discover what he was . . . a werewolf, forever doomed to metamorphosing at each full moon into the wolfish creature who had taken her so savagely and who, last night, had raked her with his claws and tasted her blood, she was nevertheless deeply relieved to know that it was he and no other who had come to her in the guise of the man-beast and lain with her.

For a long moment following her accusation, the O'Neill was silent. Finally, he spoke bleakly, dully.

"Aye, 'twas I, Sionna," he confessed, his dark visage ravaged with anguish. "And how you must despise me for that! Oh, God! I am accursed—moonstruck!—and despite all my hopes to the contrary, the madness worsens! Less easily every month am I able to curb the werewolf within me. I might have killed you, Sionna! Perhaps next time, I shall . . . " His voice broke, trailed away; and releasing her, he turned away, burying his face in his hands as he struggled to compose himself. Then, running his fingers raggedly through his shaggy hair, he continued despondently, heartsore.

"I thought if I rode you nightly, 'twould be enough to hold the werewolf at bay, to keep him from you on that one night a month when the full moon rises in the sky and the madness comes upon me. But it has not proved so; and now, I know that you will ever draw me—just as my mother drew my father. Neither iron chains nor a barred dungeon will keep me from you. I will end up growing more and more bestial until I slay you as my father slew my mother!"

Sionna gasped, stricken by this revelation. But lost in his grisly, heartrending memories, the O'Neill did not hear, and so went on with his tale.

"She was not a Kilclare, but an O'Neill of Clandeboye, a distant kinswoman. You are the first Kilclare bride of an O'Neill, Sionna. Others of your ilk taken captive in the past had a far less pleasant fate,

I fear. They were held prisoner, kept as whores for those accused, like me. At each full moon, such women would be bathed and perfumed with a special fragrance to attract the werewolf, and drugged with opiates and aphrodisiacs to make them acquiescent. Then they were given to him in his dungeon—there is a special cell in the far tower where those who are accursed spend the night of the full moon—to sate his cravings, so our own women would be safe. We had learned over the years, you see, that the werewolf eventually destroyed his Kinclare victims, as my father destroyed his. The next month, before another woman could be obtained, he broke free of his bonds in the dungeon and attacked my poor mother, killing her. After that, he went totally berserk with the moon-madness, at each full moon for three months afterward managing to escape from the dungeon. He ravaged the castle and the countryside horribly, committing rape and mayhem and murder before his men and the servants finally rose up in arms and slew him . . .

"Now, you know the truth, Sionna. I took you as my bride, knowing I could get you no other way— and how you must hate and dread me for that! Yet as God is my witness, I prayed you would be the one to rescind the curse, for I never wanted to hurt you, I swear! Though I know I have— That is why, loath though I am to part with you, I must send you away, far from Ceann-Tìre, to a nunnery, hallowed ground where you will be safe from me forever. I cannot bear to wound you further, to—to kill you, *mo miann*. I *will* not! I—I love you too much for that."

"Oh, Lucan . . . *Lucan!*" Sionna sobbed softly at this admission, tears of both joy and sorrow streaming down her cheeks.

She should despise him, she knew, for wedding her when he had known what he was, what would

become of her in his arms. His own mother had been
murdered by the father whose moon-madness he
had inherited! All his life, the O'Neill had lived with
that terrible knowledge and sorrow. Yet in truth,
Sionna's heart ached with love and pity for him; for
what more grievous burden was there for a boy to
bear or a man to endure? Aye, if she were honest,
she must admit she knew deep down inside that he
was no less a victim than she, a victim of the curse
for which he was not to blame and from which he
had sought only to save himself. They had been enemies—and how could he have guessed that love
would come to him, as it had to her, fully and for
all time?

"Oh, Lucan, what will become of you, if I agree
to go? Will not your father's fate be also your own?"

"Aye, most like. But even that I will endure for
your sake—"

"Oh, my lord, my love! . . . that you would send
me away, would give your life for my own . . . How
can I hate and dread you, knowing that? I cannot. I
cannot! I am not so cold and cruel as that, so lost in
my agony that I am immune to your own, so afraid
of your moon-madness that my love for you is not
stronger than my fear. Aye, I *do* love you, Lucan,"
she avowed as, unbidden, came the thought that if
all in the world should perish tomorrow and only
Lucan remain, she would be glad beyond her wild-
est imaginings. "With all my heart! I will not let you
send me away. I will not!" Sionna dashed away her
tears. "If legend speaks truly, there is a key to unlock
the curse, and, together, we will find it, somehow,
some way, I swear!"

"Beloved," the O'Neill uttered fiercely, taking her
in his arms and kissing her feverishly. "Oh, my beloved! Never in a million years did I think to find
your like, did I believe that you would ever come

to love me. That you can find it in your heart to do
so, especially knowing what I am—'tis like a dream
... a dream from which I do not wish to awaken
... How I thank God that you are mine! Perhaps you
are right, and, together, we can solve the riddle of
the curse. Only, promise me this, Sionna: that if we
cannot, you *will* go to a faraway convent and remain
there until I am dead—"

"Nay, oh, nay, do not speak so—"

"Shhh, hush. I must—and now, while I am strong
and sane—lest in my love for you and my madness,
I weaken in my resolve and wind up destroying you!
So on your oath, Sionna, swear to me that you will
do as I ask. Please, dear heart—for my sake."

"If 'twill please you and ease your mind, then,
aye, I do so swear," she said at last, reluctantly—
though in her heart, she vowed that it would not
come to that, not while there was breath left in her
body. Somehow, she *would* undo the curse; surely,
love would show her the way.

6

"LEAVE me!" Sionna's voice was sharp as, a
month later, she turned from the window
through which she had been staring at the full moon
and peremptorily ordered her three serving maids
from her bedchamber. "Leave me, I say!"

"But—but, my lady!" one stammered anxiously,
casting a dismayed glance at the other two. "What

about your—your bath? And—and who will help you don your nightclothes?"

"I do not require assistance," she replied coldly, knowing now how, because of their own fear, the three women had deceived and betrayed her—with their powders and perfumes and potent wine, preparing her for the werewolf who was her husband, so they and the rest of the O'Neill women would be safe. "I am not a child who must be put to bed; and as the hour is early yet and I am not tired, I would weave a while before retiring." She indicated her loom, which she had earlier that day directed two of the menservants to move to the tower, and upon which a tapestry was slowly taking shape. "However, you need not wait up, but may go to your quarters. I shall not desire your services further tonight. Now, leave me."

They would have defied her; but when she glanced pointedly at her ancestor Igrania's bewitching portrait above the hearth and then steadily back at the serving maids, her sapphire-blue eyes hard and determined, the women thought better of disobeying her instructions. Each barely dipping her a civil curtsy, they left the bedchamber—doubtless to rush to inform Cullach of her churlish behavior. Well, she would know how to deal with him, too, Sionna thought, should he be so unwise as to seek her out.

He was not, no doubt believing that the drugged wine would send her to bed soon enough. But knowing now what it contained, she did not drink it; nor did she consume any of the food on the side table. Tonight, if and when Lucan managed to escape from his bonds and the dungeon, and come to her, she must have a clear head so that if in his moonstruck madness he revealed aught of the curse to her, she would remember. That she might need her wits also to defend herself against him was a thought she determinedly shoved from her mind.

Sitting on the low stool before her loom, Sionna forced herself to concentrate on the pattern she had started to weave upon her arrival at Ceann-Tìre. But her hands stilled upon the shuttle when she heard the barking of the dogs begin, Marhalt and Maeve leading the pack. No wonder Cullach had deemed the O'Neill mad for allowing her to keep the dogs. Should they escape, they would be capable of tracking him, even of rending him limb from limb, such was their great size and strength. Sionna shuddered at the thought, for the first time glad the wolfhounds were securely chained in the kennels. In response to the dogs rose the distant howling of the wolves on the mainland and then the much-nearer lament of the one she now knew was the O'Neill, become a werewolf with the rising of the full moon in the night sky. Presently, she heard the door slam as Cullach left the donjon to feed the dogs, raw meat untainted by opiates, which the wolfhounds and Lucan would have sniffed out and instinctively refused. For knowing now why the meat upon Ceann-Tìre's tables was always cooked so rare, Sionna also understood that Cullach would offer the lion's share of the fresh kill to Lucan, in the hope of sating his many hungers.

Sionna quickly stood and moved to the window to look down upon the inner ward below. There, she saw Cullach unlock and open the door to the dungeons, which were located in a far tower. He carried the platter laden with meat. Several long minutes later, her breath caught in her throat as she heard Cullach cry out in agony; and then, to her dread, she observed the door of the tower dungeon flung wide to reveal Lucan, turned now into a werewolf, silhouetted in its frame. For an instant, the wolfish creature stood poised on the threshold—naked, magnificent, lethal, a perfect blend of a lithe, powerful man and an equally lithe, powerful beast. Throwing back his dusky, handsome head, he wailed fearsomely at the moon that was the source of his madness, then loped away into the darkness, running silently, gracefully—wild and free. He was coming, Sionna thought, abruptly frightened despite her love for him. And Cullach was hurt, perhaps even dead . . .

Not pausing to think, she grabbed up her sable mantle and raced from the bedchamber, down the spiral staircase to the O'Neill's study. There, she was relieved to find his *claidheamh mór*, as she and Lucan had earlier planned in case she should need it for protection. With both hands, she snatched up the heavy, sheathed sword, though she had no intention of hurting her husband, much less of killing him. Then she ran on, down through the great hall and out the donjon into the night. Warily, she glanced about as the door to the keep banged shut behind her, but Lucan was nowhere to be seen. Her fear allayed a little, her boots padding softly upon the cobblestones, she hurried toward the dungeons. Once inside the far tower, Sionna cautiously climbed the stone steps that wound up to the top story. As she slowly pushed open the door to the circular, torchlit chamber, she spied the stone wall that stretched across the middle of the room, dividing it in half. Set into the wall's center, she saw the stout, iron-grilled oak door that stood open, revealing the heavy iron chains embedded in the far wall. This was Lucan's prison, where he was shackled at sundown on the night of the full moon. Her heart felt sore at the sight. But there was no time for more than a glance, a moment of pity; for before the open cell, Cullach lay upon the floor. At the sight of his prone figure, Sionna relinquished her grasp on the sword; it slipped with a clatter to the floor.

"Cullach! Thank God, you are alive!"

"What—what do you here, my—my lady?" he gasped, shocked, as she hastened to his side and, kneeling beside him, began feverishly to unbuckle his barbarous clan armor—already half torn away—so she could see the extent of his wounds. "Get you hence! Get you hence!" He groaned, trying vainly to push her away. "' 'Tis dangerous for you here. A . . . prisoner has escaped—"

"Aye, I know. Lucan, my husband—the werewolf." She yanked away his steel breastplate and pulled off his gauntlets, tossing the armor aside, her brow knitted with concern as she observed the deep, vicious gouges upon his chest and arms. Tentatively, she opened his torn leather shirt to probe his chest and abdomen for any internal injury and, to her relief, found none, though it was clear he had lost a lot of blood. "Praise the saints that the wounds are not so bad as I feared . . . Cullach, can you stand?"

"Art a witch, a sorceress, in truth!" he spat, his eyes wild as he made the ancient sign to ward off evil. "How else could you be knowing such things about Lucan?"

"' 'Tis a long story—but I am no witch, I swear! 'Twas through Lucan himself that I discovered the truth. I begged him to inform no one, not even you, of the knowledge that is now mine, for I was afraid his men and the servants would somehow learn I knew the manner of the curse and, in their fear of its becoming known beyond the walls of Ceann-Tìre and rousing the whole of Ireland to arms against them, would turn upon Lucan and me both, as they did his father. Cullach, can you stand, or nay? 'Tis not lying here until sunrise I'll be leaving you if you can get to your feet. But we must hurry, do you ken? 'Tis some other poor soul Lucan will be attacking—perhaps even slaying—if he fails to find me—"

Sionna broke off abruptly as, even now, there reached her ears the sound of wolfish howls and men's frightened cries beyond the tower dungeon. "Hurry, Cullach!"

She helped him to rise, and with his arm thrown about her shoulders for support and she dragging the O'Neill's sheathed *claidheamh mór* behind, they staggered down the spiral staircase and outside to the inner ward. There, along the outer curtain walk, they spied silhouetted against the moonlight several men shouting and fleeing for their lives, away from the gatehouse mounted above the small postern gate at the rear of the castle, whose barricades gave way to a fortified road that led down to the eastern sea.

" 'Tis Lucan," Cullach stated grimly. "He is attempting to escape from the fortress."

"But . . . why? For what purpose? That way lies only the sea—" Sionna bit her lower lip, bewildered.

"Aye, but Lucan is a strong swimmer, my lady, and when the moon-madness is upon him, he has the will and strength of ten men his size. 'Tis how he manages to break free of the chains and escape from the cell; despite how we've reinforced them, they are not strong enough to hold him. When he reaches the beach below, he will take to the sea and strike out for the main shore of Ireland . . . You must help me, my lady. To the stables to rouse the grooms, so they can saddle a horse. I must go after him—"

"Don't be a fool, Cullach! Are you as mad as Lucan? You are in no condition to ride!"

"Mayhap not, but still, I must try. I know where Lucan goes—and I am the only one who has a chance of stopping him. If I cannot, he will surely be killed—"

"*Killed!* By whom?"

"As though you don't know, witch! Do you say,

then, that you did not betray your husband to your lover . . . your lover, Ruaidhri Kilclare—who has been spying on Ceann-Tîre for months, thinking to make good his boast to slay Lucan; and who, a fortnight ago, sent a taunting message to him? A message bound with red ribbon that bore a twig of wolfsbane in its knot! A message daring Lucan to meet him on the night of the full moon, at the standing stones in the forest, where you were wed! Somehow, I tell you, Ruaidhri has discovered what Lucan is—and so, doubtless, how to kill him, as well! With a silver bullet through the heart—"

Sionna's stomach shriveled into a cold knot of fear at Cullach's words. Why had Lucan kept this terrible news from her?

"Oh, God!" she cried, distraught. "Do you think I would knowingly and willingly send Lucan to his death, Cullach? I *love* him, you fool! Faith, what is the use? I can see that you don't believe me—"

"Nay, that is the damnable hell of it, my lady. I *do*. I would have to be a blind man not to see that you speak the truth. Mayhap the moon has crazed us all—or you have bewitched me, as you have Lucan . . . Go, then. Leave me! I am but slowing you down. Go, I say! Hurry! Rouse the grooms, and quickly! Tell them to saddle Lucan's destrier, Dùbhradh, for me; he is the fastest horse in the stables. I will wait here until you return."

Sionna did as he had bidden, cursing and cuffing the grooms who cowered beneath their blankets in the stables' loft. The hostlers thought she was indeed a witch, to be out and about, unharmed, upon this night, and they fell to their knees before her, pleading for mercy. But when at last Dùbhradh was saddled and led into the inner ward, it was seen that Cullach was, in truth, too ill and weak to stand, much less to ride—and no other man was brave enough to make the attempt, fearing the stallion and fearing even more Lucan in his wolfish state. In that moment, Sionna had no care for herself, only for her husband as, ignoring Cullach's hoarse protests and the terrified cries of the grooms, she abruptly flung herself into the saddle and gathered the reins. For a moment, Dùbhradh reared and pranced dangerously. But Sionna's love gave her strength, and she hung on, urging the steed toward the gatehouse.

"Open the gates!" she demanded, her voice rising above the cool spring wind that whipped her long, unbound hair, so that mounted upon the O'Neill's bold black horse, his sheathed sword slung around the saddle's pommel, she appeared like an avenging angel of darkness, the witch, the sorceress that the O'Neill's men believed her to be. That she should be in possession of both his destrier and his claymore—the two most important things on which a man depended for his life—convinced them of her power. "Open the gates—or I swear I shall curse you as did my ancestor Igrania of Clare Caiseal!" she shouted.

The men's terror was so great that they did as she commanded. In moments, she was through the gates and across the drawbridge, thundering headlong down the narrow causeway into the moonlit night.

Up the steep, treacherous, serpentine track, Sionna galloped, and across the sweeping moors, as though the hounds of hell harried her heels. Dùbhradh's hooves thudded deeply into the rich, dewy earth, churning up clumps of turf and sending them flying; and still she lashed the animal to a faster pace, hearing in her mind the whisper of sand through an hourglass and driven to recklessness by the fear that she would arrive too late, that even now, Lucan lay dead or dying, his life's blood pouring out of him at vengeful Ruaidhri's feet.

For a moment, some spark of sanity flared in her

brain, and she almost turned back; for what was she, a mere woman, against a werewolf and Ruaidhri? Then she felt the wind-borne spindrift kiss her lips, and she thought again of Lucan, who had also kissed her; and her heart was like a seabird swooping across the night sky. Heedlessly, she galloped on, knowing again the wild, fearsome thrill that had gripped her when Lucan had ridden with her through the storm. Tears born of her memories and the wind blurred her eyes, so that, at first, she could see naught but a sprawling, amorphous shadow ahead. Eventually, it delineated itself as the forested vale wherein the standing stones rose, and she pressed toward it. As she entered the woods, low-hanging boughs and greening brambles tore at her hair and scratched her skin; but still, she did not slow Dùbhradh.

At long last, Sionna came to the glade, that pagan place of the ancient standing stones; and there, bursting from the fringe of the black-cloaked trees, she drew up short at the sight that met her eyes. Lucan stood at one end of the monolith that lay at the heart of the stone ring; and for the first time, she saw him clearly in the guise of the werewolf, her mind unclouded by opiates and aphrodisiacs. He did indeed resemble the druids, the shapeshifters of old; for as they had used to do, he had cloaked his naked body with the skin of a huge black wolf, its head set upon his, so his own golden eyes looked out from the beast's empty sockets, glowing with a man's intelligence and madness and cunning. The pelt's forearms covered his own; his hands were slipped into its front paws; the rest of the hide swept down his back, the rear legs and tail dangling to the ground, so it seemed that the wolf skin was a part of him, that he had in fact metamorphosed into the beast. Even the part of him that was unconcealed seemed to have taken on a wolfish cast, the animal magnetism he had always exuded stronger, more powerful; the animal stealth and grace with which he had always moved even more menacing. Growling low in his throat, he was poised to spring upon his prey, Ruaidhri, who stood at the other end of the monolith, holding in his hands an iron harquebus. Its short, thick match cord glowed red in the darkness, ready to fly forward upon the release of its spring and to descend into the gun's pan, igniting the gunpowder that would propel the bullet from the barrel. The harquebus was pointed straight at Lucan's heart, and it was this—and only this—that held him at bay.

Sionna cried out as she scrambled haphazardly from the saddle and began to run toward them; she was within reach of Ruaidhri when Lucan lunged forward. Ruaidhri instinctively discharged the heavy gun, even as Sionna reached him and struggled to gain control of the weapon. There was a blinding flash of fire as the gunpowder caught flame; the silver ball that exploded from the barrel gleamed in the moonlight as it sped toward its intended target and struck Lucan's charging body, causing him to cry out, a wolfish howl of pain, and then to stagger back, stunned. Blood spurted from the wound in his massive chest; he crumpled slowly to the ground and lay still, the fur of the wolf pelt that covered his body rippling in the wind.

"Lucan!" Sionna screamed hysterically as her heart seemed suddenly to plunge over the edge of a yawning abyss. "Lucaaan!"

Tears rained down her cheeks. Sobbing, she would have run to her fallen husband. But flinging away the spent harquebus, Ruaidhri seized her roughly about the waist, his murderous visage tortured with hate and jealousy at the love for her husband that was plain upon her face.

"Whore!" Ruaidhri spat, giving her a savage shake. "He was a brute, a beast, accursed! You are a whore, that you came to like it in his arms, that you would weep for him!"

Bloodlust roiled within Ruaidhri yet; he leered at Sionna, making her recall his brazen boast on the night of her wedding, that he would take her beside Lucan's body. Like a wild, mad animal, she strove to break free of his bruising grip, her arms flailing as she pummeled him about the head and shoulders, and raked him viciously with her nails. But she could not escape. At last, he struck her in the face, a hard blow that sent her sprawling. In moments, he was upon her; and this, she knew she could not bear. She would rather die than be forced to yield to him. She told him as much, but he only laughed. And then, suddenly, a shadow fell upon them where they lay, and in the moonlight, the rune-engraved blade of a *claidheamh mór* glimmered silver as its point came to rest against Ruaidhri's neck.

"Get up!" It was a low-voiced snarl, a snarl that made Sionna's heart leap in her breast. "Get up, Ruaidhri, and draw your sword. My blood is yet warm—but not, I think, in the way you had intended when you sought to lay claim to what is mine."

It was Lucan, not dead, but alive—and somehow sane; for he no longer wore the wolf pelt, and though his tawny eyes were deadly, they were clear and steady. The moon-madness had apparently fled from him at the impact of the silver bullet, which had only wounded him, Sionna now saw, to her great joy and relief. Her struggle for control of the harquebus had spoiled Ruaidhri's aim; the ball had buried itself in Lucan's shoulder instead of his heart. Blood dripped down his chest from the injury; but he was an extremely strong man, and she thought that the wound would not prove mortal if she could only staunch the bleeding.

There was no time for that. Releasing her, Ruaidhri got slowly to his feet and drew his sword; and in moments, the lethal battle was joined as the clash of blade upon blade rang out in the clearing. As though possessed of an otherworldly power that shimmered and streaked silver in the moonlight, the swords flew, cut slithering swathes and arcs in the air, and came together, clattering and spitting sparks, only to disengage again and yet again. How long the duel lasted, Sionna did not know; it seemed an eternity before Lucan growled, "Now, 'tis finished, in truth!"—and took Ruaidhri's head.

Gasping and turning away from the grisly sight, Sionna cried, "Lucan!" and ran to him, felt his strong arms close about her, his mouth claim hers hungrily, speaking for him all the words in his heart. And her own heart responded fiercely as she clung to him, kissing him back with a love and passion to match his own.

Somewhere in the silence of the night, a wolf howled longingly of its desire, and its mate answered, a cry of love that was beautiful, everlasting.

"'Tis the first time since I was a lad that I have beheld a full moon and not had the madness come upon me," he marveled quietly, after a long while. "'Twill never come again, I am thinking. Because of your love, my life was spared, and the silver bullet that would have killed me instead cured me. You have ended the curse, *mo miann, a ghràidh.*" As though confirming his words, the voices of the two wolves now rose as one, forever entwined, forever loving and faithful, a sound that would never again haunt the two who listened intently to the sweet, aching echo on the wind. "They mate for life, you know," he told her as he gently lifted her in his arms and carried her to his waiting horse.

"That's because they are the wisest of creatures, *mo gràdh*," she said.

On the far horizon, the full moon slowly evanesced in the paling sky as, together, Lucan and Sionna rode toward the castle in the distance. Ceann-Tìre. Land's End—and a place of new beginning.

Gaelic Glossary

ach, ăch, *interj.* oh! alas!

a ghràidh, a grâ-igh', *n. m.* my beloved, my darling, my dear.

cailin, ca'l'-in, (English: colleen), *n. f.* lass, maid, girl.

caiseal, kăsh'-al, (English: castle), *n. m.* castle.

Ceann-Tìre, kyann-tiēru, *n. m.* peninsula, headland, promontory (lit. "Land's End").

claidheamh mór, clyiv mor, (English: claymore), *n. m.* a broadsword.

Cullach, coola, (English: Cullough), *n.* a man's Christian name.

Dùbhradh, dooru, *n. m.* shadow (the name of the O'Neill's destrier).

Lucan, loocan, *n.* a man's Christian name and an Irish placename (as in "Earl of").

mo bean-bainnse, mo ben-bén-sh, *n. f.* my bride.

mo gràdh, mo grâ-gh', *n. m.* my love.

mo miann, mo miün, *n. m.* my desire, inclination, will, love, delight, appetite.

Ruaidhri, rory, (English: Roderick, Rory), *n.* a man's Christian name, meaning "famous ruler" or "red-haired."

sgian-dubh, sciun-doo, *n. f.* a dagger, a knife (lit. "black knife").

Sionna, shanna, (English: Shanna), *n.* a woman's Christian name (from Sean, the Irish *ver.* of John), meaning "the Lord is favored, gracious, or merciful."

Tadhg, tog, *n.* a man's Christian name.

tànaiste, tānishtu, (English: tanist), *n. m.* the second-in-command, the heir.

tòiseach, tōsh'-ach, *n.* a leader, a chief.

With the exception of Christian names, all Gaelic spellings, pronunciations, and definitions in accordance with *Gaelic Dictionary (Gaelic-English, English-Gaelic; A Pronouncing and Etymological Dictionary of the Gaelic Language)* by Malcolm Maclennan [Great Britain: (published jointly by) Acair and Aberdeen University Press, 1991].

Rebecca Brandewyne

REBECCA BRANDEWYNE was born in Tennessee, but she has lived most of her life in Kansas, from where she has traveled widely, visiting many of the places about which she has written.

She was graduated *cum laude* with departmental honors from The Wichita State University, and holds a bachelor's degree in journalism, with minors in music and history, and a master's degree in communications. Before becoming a writer, she taught interpersonal communication at the university level.

She is a *New York Times* best-selling author of fourteen novels: ten historical romances, two gothics, and two fantasies. *Moonstruck* is her second novella. She has received numerous awards for her work, has millions of books in print, and is published worldwide. She is a founder and member of Novelists, Inc., a charter member of Romance Writers of America, and a member of Science Fiction and Fantasy Writers of America, Western Writers of America, and Mensa.

She resides with her husband and son in the Midwest. For a free copy of her semiannual newsletter, write to her in care of Avon Books, 1350 Avenue of the Americas, New York, New York 10019. Please enclose a stamped, self-addressed, legal-size envelope for reply.

Lovers and Demons

Shannon Drake

1

Petersburg, Virginia
1864
Under Siege

BY night, by this night, at any rate, the shells and mortar that so often hurtled toward the city, whistling their horrid cry in the air, were still.

There were no battle cries, no explosions, no screams.

The well-equipped Union Army soldiers slept, fiddled, or played mournful hamonica melodies within their camps. In the Southern trenches, the men lay back, seeking whatever rest they could find while their empty stomachs growled in terrible protest of the starvation that had seized hold of the besieged city.

In both camps, the men read letters from their loved ones, read them over and over again, folded them carefully, tenderly, and replaced them in pockets or wallets.

And in both camps, they wrote letters as well. Letters that tried to make light of the situation.

Yet letters in which all men, in blue and in gray, wondered if they would survive the next day's fighting, or perish in the blood-soaked fields and trenches.

Plaintive tunes rose on the air. So many the same from both sides.

So many weary . . . so damned sad.

Within the city, the people waited, defiant and devoted to their cause. People passionately loyal to Lee, their leader, to the belief that they must be right, that they must, in the end, win their freedom.

Yet they waited in great anguish. First through the days, then the weeks, then the months. Stalwart, they hung on. Determined, they suffered.

The pigeons had disappeared from the streets a long time ago.

Men, women, and children were all too eager for meals to question just what the meat in the pot might be—when they were so lucky to see anything that resembled meat.

The moon rose high. It was a full moon tonight.

Lenore Latham, hearing a distant, mournful song on the air, paused on her mission of mercy. She thought for a moment how much she longed to escape the war. But she couldn't run away. Her youngest brother, Teddy, just fourteen, was in the trenches surrounding the city. Her grandfather, nearly eighty, was in the trenches as well.

Her husband, Bruce, was not in the trenches. He was buried in a mass grave in Spotsylvania County where he had died well over a year ago. Sometimes, she couldn't even remember his face.

Too many faces filled her thoughts now. The drawn, terribly thin faces of little children. The desperate and also terribly thin faces of mothers. The pinched, puckered, wailing faces of infants . . .

The tortured faces of the wounded, screaming for

help, screaming for something to ease the pain . . .

No, she could never run away.

She was now attempting to move swiftly through the graveyard under the cover of the night shadows, going from kneeling angel to gentle Christ, and onward again to a large mausoleum, one that housed the deceased of a very prominent family, on her way into the blockaded city to help where she could.

She wasn't afraid of the dead. And she wasn't afraid of the cemetery. She had traveled through it often enough. But tonight, something frightened her. She held very still, and looked above her. She shivered suddenly, biting into her lower lip.

She wasn't afraid of the cemetery, but she was terrified each time she made one of her forays out of the city, seeking help from those beyond the lines of Yankees that surrounded Petersburg. But she was a native child of the place; she knew the Virginia landscape, the rivers, the forests, the plains, like few others. She even knew the cemetery she walked through now, knew many of the stones she touched, knew the old church that looked so eerily still and dark in the moonlight, knew exactly where and how she must return, time and again, to the city.

She shivered again. It seemed like such a very strange night. That full moon was rising so high in the sky, and there was a low ground fog. Soft, gray, swirling, it now misted around the old white stones of the graveyard, and around the roots of the trees, traveling upward until it seemed that the slender branches were arms with long fingers, white-bleached bone, reaching out to touch, to capture the unwary.

She gave herself a stern shake. The folks in the cemetery were beyond her help.

Others in Petersburg were not. They were desperate for the drugs and medications she was smuggling into the city. Even traveling by darkness as she did now, moving as swiftly and as furtively as possible, she carried her hoard of provisions within the fullness of her skirts—dozens of little vials tied to the wire rims of her petticoats. It had taken hours to secret them this carefully, but once she reached the city, the doctor and his desperate assistants would quickly rip them free.

She didn't have much farther to go now.

She just had to make her way through this town of the dead, and then . . .

Through the Yankee lines.

She felt a shivering seize hold of her again, and it suddenly seemed that a cloud passed over the full moon. The night was pitched into an almost total darkness, with only a few remnants of light remaining to cast a glow upon the tombstones in the cemetery, some old, some new, some toppling, some broken, some lovingly, carefully tended.

It didn't seem to matter so much now if the stones were new or old, tended or neglected. The ground fog was rising all about to cover them in mist.

From somewhere—far away? Or not so far away?—a wolf howled. The sound was long, and somehow lonely. It seemed to fade away on a shiver . . .

Lenore moistened her lips, fighting for new courage. She slipped around one of the stones and headed for the fence before the road.

Suddenly, she realized that she was not in the cemetery alone.

A shadow raced just before her, using the cloud's cover of the moon.

A shadow, someone else, some*thing* else . . .

She hung back, flinging herself behind a stone, breathing hard. Someone else could be on an errand just like her own.

The shadow had seemed so strange, not quite the shape of a man, not . . .